Maureen Peters was born in Caernarfon, North Wales. She is a prolific author and Ulverscroft has published many of her novels.

VASHTI

Tansy Clark is intrigued by the newspaper items her father shows her, about two assistant curators who have died suddenly of gastric influenza at a time when no epidemic exists. She begins her own investigation which reveals illegal and dangerous goings on behind the respectable façade of London museums. Going undercover, Tansy takes a post at a museum founded by a reclusive millionaire. But then she is attacked whilst out walking . . . Soon she is involved in a thirty-year-old story concerning the statue of a biblical queen, Vashti. Tansy must endure shocks, intrigue and a danger that bears every hallmark of death . . .

Books by Maureen Peters
Published by The House of Ulverscroft:

KATHERYN THE WANTON QUEEN
PATCHWORK
ENGLAND'S MISTRESS
WITCH QUEEN
THE LUCK BRIDE
BEGGAR MAID, QUEEN
TRUMPET MORNING

THE *VINEGAR TRILOGY:*
THE VINEGAR SEED
THE VINEGAR BLOSSOM
THE VINEGAR TREE

THE MALONE TRILOGY:
TANSY
KATE ALANNA
A CHILD CALLED FREEDOM

MAUREEN PETERS

VASHTI

Complete and Unabridged

ULVERSCROFT
Leicester

First published in Great Britain in 2006 by
Robert Hale Limited
London

First Large Print Edition
published 2007
by arrangement with
Robert Hale Limited
London

British Library CIP Data

Peters, Maureen
  Vashti.—Large print ed.—
  Ulverscroft large print series: general fiction
  1. Art museums—Employees—Death—Fiction
  2. Detective and mystery stories 3. Large type books
  I. Title
  823.9'14 [F]

  ISBN 978–1–84617–824–5

Published by
F. A. Thorpe (Publishing)
Anstey, Leicestershire

Set by Words & Graphics Ltd.
Anstey, Leicestershire
Printed and bound in Great Britain by
T. J. International Ltd., Padstow, Cornwall

This book is printed on acid-free paper

1

Autumn seemed to come more swiftly these days. Tansy hoped it wasn't a sign of rapidly advancing age. If so, there was nothing she could do about it. Instead she paused in her task to look with a mixture of satisfaction and regret at the pile of cuttings at her feet. She stood at the end of her garden, where a low wall separated the river-bank from her property. The wind had whipped up the surface of the river into whirlpools that foamed and sparkled, and at the edge of the river the grass was thick with twigs and leaves that died through green, red, gold, and orange into the sodden dark brown of their present aspect.

She heaved the mesh cage over the pile of twigs and reminded herself she would have excellent compost for the following spring. She had cut back the rose bushes hard and had the trees lopped and the grass cut by the local handyman, whose services were greatly in demand in this quiet part of Chelsea. Logs and coal were piled in the shed and the roof had been checked lest a tile came down during the winter gales.

'Miss Tansy, can you spare me a minute?'

Her housekeeper, Mrs Timothy, had come through the doors leading on to the terrace.

'Just coming!'

She bore her rake into the shed and went up the steps, pulling off her gardening boots as she entered the long sitting-room that ran from back to front of the house.

It was a pleasant room, which served also as dining-room, its walls and furniture a blend of cream and brown with accents of brilliant colour in the carpets, curtains and cushions.

'What is it, Mrs Timothy?'

She sat down to put on her shoes, casting an upward glance at the majestic figure standing before her in rustling black satin.

'It's about Tilde, Miss Tansy.' Mrs Timothy had lowered her voice.

'No problems, I hope?'

'Oh no, miss!' The other shook her head. 'Tilde and I rub along nicely. It's about the birthday.'

'If you mean mine, I've no intention of remembering it, let alone celebrating it,' Tansy said wryly.

Thirty-five, she reflected, wasn't far off forty and best left unobserved.

'Tilde's birthday, miss,' Mrs Timothy said.

'Of course! Goodness, how time flies. She

came to us when she was seventeen and that was four years ago. I agree, twenty-one is a birthday that needs a bit of notice taking of it. What would you advise?'

There was nothing Mrs Timothy liked more than being appealed to for advice. Now she beamed and said, 'I thought a nice iced cake and perhaps a visit to the theatre. You know how she goes on about that Shakespeare stuff — I cannot make head nor tail of it myself but she might enjoy seeing it spoken on a real stage. Of course, it's your decision.'

'I think she would love to visit the theatre,' Tansy said. 'I shall obtain the very best seats for you both.'

'Oh no!' Mrs Timothy looked alarmed. 'You'll pardon me, Miss Tansy, but I could not abide to sit through a play by Shakespeare. It would agitate my back something cruel!'

Since Mrs Timothy's bad back governed her activities, there was no point in trying to persuade her. Tansy said instead, 'Then I will take her to the theatre and you may bake the cake. I think I ought to increase her wages too.'

'But not by too much,' Mrs Timothy said. 'She has ideas above her station, you know. Now I'll say nothing about her birthday to her. She gets so excited at the prospect of a treat!'

Mrs Timothy made Tilde sound like a child, Tansy mused. But Tilde was an exceedingly pretty young woman, her dark hair curling naturally into long ringlets, her eyes huge in her small face. It was only by great good fortune and Mrs Timothy's strict rules that she hadn't been snapped up by a prospective husband already.

The housekeeper left the room and Tansy reached for the daily newspaper, running her eye down the closely printed columns.

The Prince of Wales was paying an official visit to India, where no doubt he would find a goodly selection of charming ladies with whom to dally. Princess Alexandra was a saint to endure it! A roller-skating rink had been opened in London.

Tansy lowered the newspaper with a little sigh. In her mind a vivid picture of herself leapt up of the days when she had been a child, bowling her hoop in the local park where her parents enjoyed an afternoon saunter, walking arm in arm, discussing the current case on which her father, Chief Inspector Laurence Clark, had been engaged. He had made a point of talking over the most interesting cases with his wife, whether or not their small daughter was there to hear about the latest bloodthirsty murder.

Theirs had been an ideal marriage, a meeting of minds, with her father eager to involve his wife as far as possible in his profession and to encourage his daughter to pick up every scrap of knowledge. There had been nothing then to warn them of how the happy years would end with her mother's death, followed within a couple of years by the bullet that had shattered her father's spine and precipitated his retirement from the force.

She picked up the newspaper again, banishing the past.

The new sewerage system was completed. She hoped that would mean a cleaner river and an end to the yearly outbreaks of cholera and typhoid. It was shameful that in this year of 1875 the great city of London should still be choked with slums, houses unfit for human occupation, courtyards and alleys running with filth. What was needed, she thought with an inward grin, was another Great Fire. She imagined herself starting it and her father quickly fastening on the culprit.

Now here was something interesting! The assistant curator at a small private museum had died quite suddenly of a gastric upset after only a brief illness. Tansy grimaced. She knew the museum quite well, having often visited it with her fiancé, Geoffrey.

For the second time she was lost in memories. Geoffrey had died of yellow fever nearly twelve years before while visiting his late father's plantation in Jamaica, only weeks before he had been due to sail home for the wedding. His will had left her the house they had chosen together during their engagement, along with a yearly income which enabled her to live in moderate comfort. Although he had drawn his income from the Jamaican estate, his real love had been for ancient artefacts, especially those of the Near East.

'After we are married we will go out there and help at a dig,' he had promised. 'You will love it!'

But that had never happened.

She wondered which of the assistant curators had died and then reminded herself that, as nearly twelve years had elapsed since she had visited the museum with Geoffrey, it was unlikely she had met him.

There was nothing else worth reading, she decided, putting the newspaper aside and rising from her seat. She had promised to dine with her father this evening, which meant she had better hurry and get changed. By the time she reached his home it would be quite dark.

She had been born in that building, had expected to be married from it, until the news had come of Geoffrey's death.

'Go and live in the house he left you,' her father had urged. 'You're an intelligent, active young women and I'm not prepared to have you waste your youth in caring for a parent who will probably be confined to a wheelchair for the rest of his life. There's nothing worse than a parent hanging on to a daughter who is quite capable of carving out a new life for herself.'

It had been unusual eleven years before, for an unmarried woman in her mid-twenties to live alone save for a couple of servants but he had insisted and eventually she had obeyed and moved into the house she and Geoffrey had decorated and furnished together before he sailed to Jamaica. It had been difficult at first because when her glance fell on some particular vase she couldn't stop herself recalling how they'd chosen it together, how they'd laughed when the curtains they'd chosen refused to stay on their rail but kept slithering down as if in defiance of their plans, but slowly she had begun to build a routine for herself which kept her busy and, as the years went by, often happy.

Occasionally she wondered that it would be

like to have to seek paid employment. She often saw young women hurrying to offices where many now worked as secretaries or shepherding small children across the road towards a school. Those women at least enjoyed a certain dignity in their employment but too many worked for a pittance in damp, overheated sweatshops where their every moment was timed and the work itself soul-destroyingly tedious. Having a private income gave Tansy the freedom to choose. She satisfied her conscience by doing a respectable amount of charity work though that consisted mainly of bothering people on their doorsteps for contributions, and in the four years since she had taken Tilde into service she had found herself inadvertently involved in two exceedingly puzzling murder cases. The hours she had spent riveted by the conversation between her parents concerning some particular crime had evidently sharpened her wits, she reflected now, going upstairs to the large bedroom with its double bed where she had once expected to sleep with Geoffrey. In the years since, she had found the ache for what might have been growing less and now she slept soundly, alternating sides.

Fashions were becoming more elaborate, the wide skirts drawn to the back in a mass of pleats and frills, hats were rapidly replacing bonnets and the Alexandra fringe was becoming popular.

Tansy, at five feet eight inches, was taller than the average woman and her extreme slenderness made her seem taller still. Her features were too strongly marked for feminine beauty and her green eyes and heavy fall of curling red hair had never been fashionable though her father assured her that one day they would be.

By which time, Tansy thought, I shall have grey hair and wear spectacles!

Amused at the picture conjured in her mind, she changed into a lacy white blouse and straight skirt of dark orange serge, and slipped on the matching jacket. Her heavy hair, caught into a snood of light brown silk, obviated the necessity for a hat, and looking at herself in the long pier glass she felt that she did indeed look rather attractive, a thought that brought a broad smile to her lips.

'Are you going out, Miss Tansy?'

Tilde, trim in her print frock and white apron, came to open the front door.

'I'm going to see my father,' Tansy informed her. 'Don't wait up for me. I have my key.'

'Mrs Timothy never feels easy until you're

home safe and sound,' Tilde said. 'With the dark evenings starting to draw in it's dangerous to be out alone.'

'Not in Chelsea it isn't,' Tansy said firmly. 'I expect to arrive in perfect safety.'

'We all hope that,' a voice concurred.

A tall figure loomed on the front path, hat in hand, fair hair glinting in the approaching sunset.

'Frank, are you come to call?' Tansy said. 'I am just setting out for my father's!'

'So am I. I was invited to dinner this morning and since Finn mentioned that you were also expected I thought we might share a cab,' he returned pleasantly.

Finn, her father's manservant, lost no opportunity when it came to matchmaking, Tansy thought, her lips twitching into a smile.

'That's nice,' Tilde observed.

'And good evening to you, Tilde,' Frank said. 'You grow prettier every time I see you.'

'Full many a flower is born to blush unseen and waste its sweetness on the desert air,' Tilde quoted.

'Chelsea isn't a desert and the day you blush unseen I emigrate!' Tansy said, amused.

'You'll have to look about for a new maidservant soon,' Frank teased. 'Or does Mrs Timothy disapprove of followers?'

'I disapprove of them myself, Mr Cartwright,' Tilde said, lifting her small chin
proudly. 'It's not a comfortable thing to be
followed home twice from the butcher's and
the greengrocer's in one week!'

'Someone followed you?'

Tansy, about to step through the front
door, turned sharply.

'Twice, Miss Tansy. On Tuesday I was
coming along the street just before supper
with a nice loin of pork and I heard footsteps
behind me. When I turned round the
footsteps stopped and I couldn't see anyone
but I reckon they stepped behind a tree. I
came on faster and looked round once or
twice but nobody was there,' Tilde said
earnestly.

'You said twice,' Tansy reminded her.

'Only yesterday at around the same time.'
Tilde nodded. 'I was coming along with the
vegetables. I forgot to buy the carrots in the
morning and Mrs Timothy said as how you'd
be quite put out if there were no carrots to go
with the beef and I said that Miss Tansy had a
soul above carrots — '

'Never mind my soul!' Tansy said impatiently. 'What happened next?'

'The same thing,' Tilde said. 'I just took to
my heels and ran. It was too foggy to see
anything clearly but I turned round when I

got to the gate and the footsteps stopped and then went the other way. I had the impression of a very sinister figure with his hat pulled low.'

Disregarding the 'sinister', which had probably had its origin in Tilde's lively imagination, Tansy asked, 'Did you mention this to Mrs Timothy?'

'Oh no, Miss Tansy! She'd only start fussing and insist on having everything delivered,' Tilde said. 'It makes a nice change for me to go shopping.'

Tansy suppressed a smile, having a shrewd suspicion that Tilde's enthusiasm for shopping had a great deal to do with the fact that the butcher's assistant was a handsome young man.

'You must run your errands earlier in the day in future,' she said aloud. 'Don't bolt the front door. I have my key.'

'And Mr Cartwright,' Tilde said, stifling a giggle as she closed the front door.

'Our Tilde's growing up,' Frank observed as they walked to the cab stand.

'She'll be twenty-one soon,' Tansy told him. 'I'm planning a surprise theatre visit for her. You know how she is forever quoting poetry and going on about Shakespeare.'

'You must be one of the nicest employers in London,' he commented.

'I like to be fair to people,' she told him.

'And what will you do when Tilde finds herself a husband and leaves?'

'I may entice Finn away from Pa and encourage him to court Mrs Timothy,' Tansy said, mock-serious. 'Pa, of course, would never forgive me!'

Laughing, they boarded the waiting cab.

★ ★ ★

In the now semi-gloom of the evening, Frank's profile appeared intermittently as the vehicle passed street lights at intervals. In his early forties he was, she thought, a handsome man, his features chiselled, his fair hair thick and smooth. Unlike many men he didn't wear a moustache and his sideburns were of reasonable length. He always looked clean and smart. Even in the office where he wrote his columns for various newspapers, his sleeves rolled up, a green eyeshade directing his gaze downward, he appeared presentable. When she looked at him, something inside her, long suppressed, stirred a little.

Reaching the large handsome house where she had spent the first part of her life and where her father still lived, she felt, as always, old memories yawning into consciousness.

Pa now spent his days largely in the

enormous first-floor sitting-room which functioned also as library and dining-room. All her pictures of childhood were centred in the panelled room with the curtains of crimson velour and the heavily gilded chandeliers now adapted to gas, the tables and chairs of mahogany with the tapestry cushions her mother had made, the prints on the walls, the bookshelves that covered two walls and the long windows that looked out across the park opposite.

She didn't even need to close her eyes to conjure up her mother, wide skirts spread around her as she sat sewing, only lifting her braided head to enquire now and then in her placid way, 'And did they find the head, dear, or merely the dismembered torso?'

Finn, opening the door to them, allowed his lugubrious features to stretch into a smile.

'Nice to see you, Miss Tansy! You too, Mr Frank!'

His own quarters were on the ground floor, as was the kitchen where he practised his culinary skills far more successfully than he had once burgled houses, until her father had offered him a job and a last chance to go straight.

'What have you prepared for dinner?' Tansy enquired, knowing he liked to vary his menus 'like a real chef, miss', and despite her

14

slenderness having a hearty appetite herself.

'Mushroom pancakes, fillet of beef in a croute, which is French for beef in puff pastry with a drop of red wine sauce,' Finn informed her.

'You spoil us,' Tansy said.

From above her father called down, 'Come up and stop gossiping with my valet!'

'Coming, Pa!'

Tansy ran lightly up the curving staircase, recalling as usual how as a child she had often delighted in sliding down the banister.

The room was bright, a fire blazing in the hearth, the gas lamps lit and the table laid with as much care as if the Queen were expected.

Laurence Clark occupied his wheelchair as usual. His spinal injury had in no way diminished the vitality that crackled from him and from his iron-grey hair — once as red as his daughter's — and mobile features.

'If I ever return to live with you, Pa,' Tansy said, taking off her jacket, 'I shall insist on a change of curtains. These clash dreadfully with my hair!'

'That's why I keep them!' her father retorted. 'Merely to prevent you from invading my peace and quiet by playing the dutiful daughter. Good evening, Frank! Glad you could come!'

'Good evening sir.' Frank smiled as he entered. 'I take it this invitation means you have a problem to solve.'

Officially retired since his wounding, Laurence Clark still took a keen interest in the crime scene and, though chair-bound, was frequently consulted by officers from the Yard eager to benefit from his experience.

'It means I looked forward to a bit of company,' Laurence retorted. 'However . . . ' he added darkly.

'However?' Tansy looked at him.

'Let's enjoy Finn's cooking first,' Laurence said provokingly, wheeling himself neatly to the table.

'Wine, sir?' Frank indicated the sideboard with its array of decanters and bottles.

'The red this evening, I think. What news are you chasing at the moment?'

'Not very much at all,' Frank said, pouring wine for them. 'London is between seasons and with the Prince of Wales abroad there's no scandal worth reporting.'

'If Her Majesty would come out of retirement that would jolt the nation,' Finn observed, arriving with the first course.

'She's too busy luxuriating in her own grief,' Laurence said cynically. 'No, as far as scandal goes I'm thinking you may have to create your own!'

16

He sent his daughter a quizzical glance which she studiously ignored though her cheeks flushed slightly.

Not, she thought, that getting together with Frank would merit even a mention in any of the newspapers! She and Frank had been friends for ever and she knew that he wanted more than the bantering friendship she permitted, but at the last moment something held her back. Perhaps the memory of Geoffrey haunted her more than she could admit.

Not until the meal had been relished, the beef succeeded by a blackberry compote, brandy and coffee had gone the rounds, and Finn had seated himself as usual on a chair which stood slightly apart from where Laurence and his guests were seated, did Tansy say, 'Come on, Pa! What have you to tell us?'

'Only a couple of items recently in the newspapers that caught my eye,' he said, reaching for his pipe. 'Nothing to it in all probability but they intrigued me.'

'Sir, your instincts are nearer to a bloodhound's than anyone I ever met,' Frank said. 'Do go on!'

'Where are those cuttings, Finn?'

'Right here, sir!'

Finn passed them over.

'Here we are!' Laurence cleared his throat. 'September the fifteenth. 'The death is announced of Mr Joseph Fanshaw, assistant curator of the Royston Museum. Mr Fanshaw was taken ill a week ago and died of gastric fever yesterday. He was thirty years old and leaves no family. The funeral will be private.' '

'And?' Frank looked puzzled.

'Today the death was reported of a Mr Brook Wilton — '

'Assistant curator of the Kensington Museum.' Frank nodded.

'Brook Wilton was twenty-seven years old and leaves no family.'

'Coincidence?' Tansy hazarded.

'Two young, apparently healthy men, no relatives, both working at the same jobs, both died of gastric fever in autumn when there have been no reports of any infectious outbreaks anywhere? Doesn't that give you pause for reflection?'

He looked from one to the other.

18

2

Tansy, watching, felt a stir of excitement. Her father studied the newspapers closely and had an almost photographic memory. The first case in which she had become involved had begun with an advertisement in the personal column from someone signing themselves Valentine. The second had arisen from the report of a man found in the river. In both cases she had faced danger before the culprits had been apprehended.

'Perhaps they caught the illness because they frequent the same restaurants,' Frank said. 'Food does go off if the weather's warm.'

'Not in this 'ouse!' Finn said staunchly.

'And it wasn't that hot last month either,' Laurence said.

'The Royston Museum is in Chelsea, by the way.'

Frank looked at Tansy.

'I've passed it once or twice but I don't think I've ever been in,' she said. 'It looks rather gloomy.'

'Anyway, it doesn't sound particularly suspicious to me,' Frank added.

'Not on the surface.' Laurence drank his

brandy. 'It's an odd coincidence though and where there are odd coincidences I look for links, for some common denominator.'

'Which we already have,' Tansy put in. 'Two young men, both without relatives, both working in museums, both dying suddenly.'

'Did they know each other?' Frank asked.

'I have no idea.' Laurence shrugged his broad shoulders. 'Do assistant curators mingle socially, I wonder?'

'I would have thought that most museums and galleries were in hot competition with one another,' Frank said. 'Each one wants to own something the others haven't got, something that will bring in the crowds. Do we know who owns the Kensington Museum?'

'The council, I believe.'

'And the Royston?'

'Carl Royston. In his eighties by now, I daresay,' Laurence said.

'Who is Carl Royston?' Tansy enquired. 'The name sounds familiar.'

Geoffrey might have mentioned it, she thought suddenly.

'He inherited the Royston millions when I was a young man,' Laurence said. 'He spent much of it on various community-minded projects — gold and diamond shares passed down from his father so possibly he felt slightly guilty as he had so much and others had so little. Orphans, fallen women, that kind of thing.'

'Funny 'ow they always call 'em 'fallen', ain't it?' Finn remarked. 'In my young days, begging your pardon, Miss Tansy, they was usually up and running for it.'

'Anyway, he lives in a house over in Park Lane,' Laurence continued, stifling a chuckle. 'A widower. I believe there's a son. Years back we had to investigate a robbery there. Some coins were taken — '

'Not yours truly,' Finn put in. 'I never went in for coins. Not easy to fence.'

'If ever I decide to embark on a criminal career I'll bear that in mind,' Frank observed.

'Did they find the thief?' Tansy enquired.

'A footman,' her father said. 'Very swiftly found, arrested and the coins recovered. He'd actually been trying to sell them down at Covent Garden. Mr Royston refused to press charges on the grounds that he didn't want his ownership of such valuables to become general knowledge and very likely attract further thefts, and the matter was dropped.'

'You met Mr Royston then?' Frank asked.

'Yes, indeed, on several occasions. Good-looking, intelligent and obviously cultured — '

He paused, frowning slightly.

'But?'

Tansy looked a question.

'He had a cool, calculating manner,' Laurence said slowly. 'Of course, I was pretty low down in the Force then but I liked to make up my mind independently about people and I can recall thinking him a cold fish under the politeness.'

'What happened to the footman?' Frank asked.

'I presume he was dismissed with a very lukewarm character reference,' Laurence said. 'As no charges were brought the case was closed, especially as the coins were quickly recovered.'

'And what was he like? The footman?' Tansy enquired.

'I didn't get to question him, being a junior officer at the time,' Laurence told her.

'And you really think the perfectly natural deaths of these two men need looking into?' Frank said.

'Their deaths were apparently natural,' Laurence stressed, 'but, yes, I do have a strong feeling that something isn't quite right.'

Tansy, watching the play of expression over his strong-boned face, recognized the look. It meant that years of patient observation allied to a quick mind had joined together as they had in the past and it meant that since

Laurence was wheelchair-bound, the legwork would have to be done by herself and Frank, with Finn hovering in the background.

'I'll see what I can find out,' Frank said.

'And I'll have a look round the two museums,' Tansy added.

'Where did those two assistant curators live?' Frank asked, producing his pocket-book and a pencil.

'No addresses given,' Laurence told him.

'The coroner's office will have a record,' Frank said. 'I take it there was an inquest?'

'Apparently not — nothing about any inquest in the newspapers anyway. If the doctors both certified natural causes due to gastric fever there would have been no necessity. I daresay neither man had a fortune to leave, even if there were any relatives waiting to claim it.'

'I'll make some enquiries anyway.' Frank replaced his pocketbook and pencil.

'It may all be perfectly innocent,' Laurence said, sounding as if he was trying to convince himself.

'But you hope that it isn't!' Tansy gave her father a comradely grin and nodded towards Finn to bring her jacket. 'I shall visit the Royston Museum as soon as possible. It's quite near so I can probably do that tomorrow morning.'

'Just get a general idea of the place,' he said, nodding.

'I pass it several times a week but I've never seen anybody going in or out,' Tansy said.

'His philanthropic actions didn't bear fruit then,' Laurence mused. 'If the old gentleman's still alive — see if you can find out.'

'I could apply for a job there or go round collecting for one of my charities,' Tansy said, pleased at the prospect of action. 'Finn, that was a delicious meal!'

'And it won't give nobody gastric fever,' Finn said.

'Good night, sir.' Frank was also rising.

'Stay and talk men's talk with Pa,' Tansy said.

She was aware of the great admiration Frank had for the older man and the interest Laurence took in the journalist. It was not merely that their tastes and ideas often agreed. Though he had never mentioned the subject to her, Tansy was aware that he knew very well, without a word being uttered, that Frank's affection for her had passed beyond friendship and that she herself was trying desperately to keep it in check. Never once had Laurence invited her to confide in him about her innermost feelings and for that she was grateful because she would have hesitated to define them even to herself.

'Not until I've seen you safely into a cab,' Frank answered now. 'I'll be back in ten minutes or less, sir.'

He seized his hat as Finn held open the door

Going down the stairs, Tansy said on a spurt of laughter, 'When I was small I used to long for the day when I'd be big enough to slide down these banisters and when I reached the right age I didn't really want to do it any longer!'

'A pleasure deferred is a gift refused,' Frank said.

He had crooked his arm and she slipped her own hand through it as they crossed the street towards the park opposite.

'Do you think Pa has something solid in his suspicions?' she enquired.

'It could be that he's bored,' Frank considered. 'Tied down as he is, he must feel frustrated at times, but on the other hand he has a sure instinct for what may be a crime.'

'Not that way!' Tansy said involuntarily as they entered the park and Frank turned to the left.

She had spoken without thinking and at once sensed the stiffening of the arm through which her hand was tucked.

'Something wrong?' Frank stopped and looked at her by the light of a gas jet at the edge of the path.

'Nothing,' she said hastily. 'I wasn't thinking, that's all. You know it was here I first found Tilde just four years ago — newly unemployed, deeply depressed and quite ready to drown herself in a couple of feet of water! We have laughed about it since but she is as romantic as ever she was!'

'And the park's mixed up with your memories of Geoffrey,' Frank said, steering her neatly through the gates on to the pavement again. 'You told me once that he proposed to you there.'

'By the lilac bush,' Tansy said.

The purple and white candles of the lilac had been out, filling the air with their scent. She had paused to breathe in the perfume, thinking, she remembered, that fascinating as old and beautiful objects were, there was nothing to compare with the scent of living flowers, and Geoffrey had swung her around to face him and asked her to be his wife and kissed her by the explosion of lilacs when she had accepted.

Only later had she recalled the old superstition that lilacs were an unlucky flower, laid in olden times on the biers of the dead, but when she had mentioned it to Geoffrey he had said calmly, 'Silly superstitions were meant to be defied.'

26

So they had defied them and Geoffrey had sailed off to see about his father's estate and died of yellow fever there.

'A penny for them,' Frank said now as they paced the lamplit pavement that half circled the park.

'I was just wishing you had known Geoffrey,' Tansy said. 'He was such a civilized man, very clever but good at explaining things, and interested in so many subjects. You would have liked him.'

'It's possible,' Frank said. There was a hint of weariness in his voice.

'I'm sorry! I don't mean to go on talking about him. I don't often drag him into the conversation, do I?'

'He's usually there whether you mention him or not,' Frank said. 'Hanging round like a guest at a party who should have gone home ages ago!'

'That's not fair!' she said indignantly.

'All right, you don't often talk about him but you always manage to make other people aware of his importance to you after — How many years ago did he die?'

'Nearly twelve years,' she said in a small voice.

She had just finished having her wedding dress fitted. Creamy satin with a wide-spreading skirt and sleeves bordered with lace

27

to match the trimming on her short veil.

When the dreadful news had come she had received it with outward calm but inside she had felt a tearing desolation.

'Let me know when you've decided to let go of him,' Frank said abruptly. 'Here's a cab!'

He waved it down impatiently.

'Frank, we're not quarrelling, are we?' she asked.

'No, just being honest. You shouldn't spend your life living in the past. Night, Tansy!'

He kissed her briefly on the cheek, closed the cab door behind her and walked off, his gait suggesting impatience.

Tansy gave her address to the cabbie and sat back, indignation surging up in her. It really wasn't fair to suggest that she was always or even sometimes bringing Geoffrey into the conversation. Then she recalled an elderly neighbour who had once lived near them. She had been in her late fifties and might have been pretty once, save that her face bore a settled look of resigned sadness, and when Tansy had paused politely to wish her good day the woman had always sighed gently and murmured that it looked like rain.

'Lost her fiancé at Waterloo,' Laurence had said briskly when Tansy made enquiry of him. 'Nearly sixty years ago and she still dwells on it in her mind even though she hardly ever mentions his name. Sad and stupid because life goes on whatever changes.'

And life had gone on for her, Tansy decided, but Frank had been wrong about her living in the past. The truth was that her heart was clinging on to something that was becoming increasingly indistinct in her mind.

She found it difficult to recall Geoffrey whole and entire, or to remember the sound of his voice or the touch of his hand. She could only grasp at him in bits and pieces like a picture that has fragmented with time.

She felt guilty about that because it was thanks to Geoffrey's legacy that she lived an independent life with two servants in a charming little house.

She rapped on the roof as the cab turned a corner.

'Here will do nicely. Thank you!'

Stepping down, proffering the fare and adding a tip, she was conscious of the cabbie's face as he leaned down — a broad red face with a smile that widened into a grin when he saw the size of the tip. She wondered if he too had some painful memory to forget.

'You all right, ma'am? Fog's rolling in,' he observed.

'I don't live very far from here and Chelsea

is fairly safe, I think,' she returned pleasantly and stood back as he urged the horses on again.

It was indeed quite dark by now, the moon obscured by the drifting fog. In the centre of town the fog would be thicker and yellower, mixed with soot and foul smelling. Here there was at least the pleasant illusion of being in the country with the houses and gardens neatly spaced out and the Thames flowing past between banks still fringed with tall grasses and wild flowers.

It was one of her delights to sit on her back wall in late summer afternoons and watch the fishing boats and the little pleasure steamer that chugged up and down with visitors crowded aboard.

Even walking along the pavement one could see sections of the river between the houses, like pale washes of colour meeting the sky in some painting or other. The river had its sinister side too. Boats rowed by women were ferried past the weir with its great wheel and long hooks used to hoist out the debris thrown in by careless passers-by. Occasionally a body was dragged out with grappling hooks and neighbours closed their back curtains or came out to watch, according to their liking of such spectacles.

Along the road itself the gas jets gleamed

but the fog was settling a blanket over the roofs of the houses, drifting like grey lace across the darkening water where a ripple of silver still broke the surface from time to time.

From the pavement one couldn't see the waterwheel on which she had once seen with horror the figure of a murdered man tied.

She remembered that image even without closing her eyes, remembered the sick feeling that surged into her throat like the swill from the dirtier section of the river. Now, recalling also the risks she had run in order to bring a killer to justice, she wondered if this latest newspaper item, or rather two of them, would open up something she would prefer to forget later on.

Whatever the outcome, she wasn't sure that Frank would appreciate her entering again the rarefied world of antiques where she and Geoffrey had spent so many happy hours browsing as he tried to explain the subtle differences between one artefact and another, or pointed out that a carving she had guessed to be hundreds of years old was in fact a fake, artificially distressed and still quite valuable but, like some people, not exactly what it seemed to be.

At least she could rely on Frank never changing, she mused, thinking with pleasure of his undemanding friendship. Then her feet slowed and stopped because it occurred to her with a little shock of insight that she was deceiving herself. Frank had begun to make it increasingly plain that a platonic relationship was becoming less and less to his taste. He was too much of a gentleman to make outright demands but this evening his irritable remark about Geoffrey had betrayed deeper feelings.

She could have invited Frank in for a cup of coffee before he returned to her father's. Laurence never minded staying up late for a conversation about crime and Finn had always been a night owl. She could have given him a little more encouragement even though part of her was still clinging to a past that would never come again.

She resumed her slow pace, passing the open spaces beyond which glimpses of the river could be seen through the thickening fog.

It was then that she heard the footsteps, walking slowly some yards behind her, muffled by the fog and disregarded by her own churning thoughts. Tansy stopped abruptly and the footsteps abruptly ceased.

She frowned slightly, took a few paces forward and heard the footfalls again, keeping pace just one heartbeat behind her own, pausing when she paused a second time.

She risked a quick glance behind her but the pavement curved at this time and a tall sycamore leaned out to conceal anyone waiting in its deeper shadow.

She had been a fool, she decided, to dismiss the cab so readily in the hope that a walk would clear her thoughts. They were as muddled as ever and she was conscious of the emptiness of her surroundings with the curtains behind the windows of the houses drawn across and the garden gates closed save where one flapped idly to and fro on its guarding post.

She stepped briefly inside, drawing the gate shut with her left hand, herself concealed by the thick laurel bush that spread itself across half the path within. She didn't know the people who lived here — a retired couple she believed — who might perhaps be unnecessarily alarmed if a completely strange woman begged for an escort home.

In any case, the footsteps had ceased completely and might even have been echoes of her own tread as she walked. The fog too distorted sounds.

She stepped back through the gate and walked a little more quickly, hearing again the footfalls behind which steadily gathered pace like some threatening echo.

There was no sense in running. Nevertheless she found her own strides had increased in length and in speed, her long legs under her skirt covering the ground rapidly, her heart hammering so loudly in her ears that she was not aware for a moment or two that the footfalls keeping pace with hers had stopped altogether, a circumstance that made her feel more rather than less apprehensive.

She had reached her own gate, gone swiftly up the path and had just taken out her key when Tilde opened the front door.

'I was in the sitting room just now and I saw you from the front window, miss,' the girl said.

'It's late, Tilde.' Tansy tried to catch her breath. 'I told you not to wait up.'

'I know, miss, but Mrs Timothy was reminiscing about when she was a girl and we had an extra cup of tea and then I came into the sitting room because I forgot earlier to draw the curtains and the fog was floating about and making the strangest shapes that it was fascinating to watch,' Tilde explained.

Not to mention the fact that the butcher's boy occasionally walked past after a long day's labour, Tansy thought, her lips twitching. Aloud she said, 'Did you notice anyone walking past the house.'

'Only you, miss, and you opened the gate

and came up the path. Why?'

'No reason,' Tansy said. 'Is the kettle still on the hob?'

'It's always on the hob,' Tilde said simply.

'Make me a cup of tea and then take yourself off to bed,' Tansy instructed.

She must take care not to let her imagination run away with her in future, she decided, as she sat down by the still glowing fire.

It had been imagination, hadn't it?

3

There was no point in lying awake half the night worrying about what might not have been! Tansy summoned her usual common sense and, having drunk her tea, rechecked the locks on doors and windows and took herself off to bed. Yet it was surprisingly difficult to settle herself. The bedroom, which with its adjoining bathroom was directly above her sitting room, seemed to be fuller of shadows than usual as if memories themselves held the contours of feelings long passed.

Tansy got up twice to check the windows again, looking out to see nothing more alarming than the bushes lining the front path waving to and fro and the river at the back lit by a Jacob's-ladder that alternated silver with black and was frequently imprisoned in the mist.

Finally she slept fitfully and late, waking to find Tilde standing at the foot of the bed with coffee on a tray and her pretty face filled with alarm.

'Good morning, Tilde.' Tansy hoisted herself into a sitting position. 'What time is it?'

36

'Past 9.30, miss,' Tilde said, relief lighting her expression. 'I was beginning to worry and Mrs Timothy was all for coming up to investigate except that her back has been playing her up something cruel, so I said I'd come and find out why you hadn't rung your bell. You know my mother told me once that when she lived in Paris she had a friend who went to bed one night and died in her sleep but the strange thing was that her bell continued to ring!'

'So as mine didn't ring you deduced I was still alive,' Tansy said, amused.

'Hope,' said Tilde solemnly, 'springs eternal in the human breast.'

With which she retreated, leaving Tansy to relish her coffee and to make herself presentable for church.

★   ★   ★

The church itself was within walking distance and was the place she and Geoffrey had decided to hold their nuptials since it was near the house they had chosen and decided to live in after their honeymoon. She never entered the church without seeing in her mind's eye the misty might-have-been of herself walking slowly up the aisle but this morning that vision was overlaid by the picture of two separate funerals, both of assistant curators who had died quite suddenly of gastric fever, left no relatives and been buried with only her father noting the curious coincidence.

Sunday lunch was always a roast, Mrs Timothy being of the opinion that only roast meat was suitable fare for the Lord's Day. She and Tilde usually attended the early evening service, which meant that the lunch was always hot and savoury. Tansy, having decided during the sermon upon a plan of action, praised the lamb and the baby vegetables, agreed with Tilde that the syllabub was just nicely flavoured with lemon and took herself upstairs where, after a little thought, she changed into one of her plainer dresses of dull green with a short, fitted jacket trimmed with black braid over a plain white blouse. Women who went collecting for charity or hoped to find employment generally wore bonnets rather than hats. She tied on a bonnet of the same sombre green as the dress, checked that she had the necessary identification in her reticule and sallied forth.

Today the fog lingered here and there, its greyness shot through with a nimbus of gold, as the early autum sun gilded the afternoon. As she walked to the cab-stand Tansy kept her eyes open for anything that might lend weight to her impressions of the previous night but apart from several decaying branches hanging limply from some of the trees there was nothing to hint at following footsteps or someone concealing themselves when she had paused to look behind her.

'The Royston house in Park Lane,' she instructed the cab driver. 'Do you know it?'

'Yes, ma'am. The millionaire gentleman lives there,' she was informed.

The house itself, which she must have passed at other times without paying it particular heed, stood at the junction of the road, other dwellings of some status surrounding it. The Royston house, she thought, having paid the fare and stepped out on to the pavement, was a three-storey mansion with a courtyard before it behind high gates. Its façade was plain, curtains of plain white net obscuring the windows though here and there a heavier drape of grey velvet had been closely drawn. The courtyard itself held no fountain or flower pot. This was a building that didn't seek to impress a passer-by, she mused, pushing open one side of the gate.

It was also a house in which the owner would think long and hard before he parted with a penny to any casual charity worker.

Changing her mind about her original plan, she crossed the courtyard, mounted the steps and rang the doorbell.

The front door, which was of plain, polished oak with a discreet knocker of beaten copper, swung open and a tall, thin footman stood within.

'Miss Tansy Clark to see Mr Royston,' she said, rather more boldly than she felt.

'Wait here, please.'

He stood aside to allow her to enter a high, wide hall, indicating a chair set in an alcove, then he vanished, in the silent manner of his kind, through double doors on the left.

Tansy looked round at the panelled walls with the small shields mounted on alternate panels, at the staircase that curved up towards a small gallery and at the white netted windows. This was a severely masculine dwelling with no sign of a flower or a pretty landscape. The only other article of furniture in the hall was a hallstand with silver tipped antlers to hold coats and hats but the antlers gleamed bare in the slight gloom and indicated that few went out or came in.

'Who? What does she want?'

The voice, issuing from the half-open doors on the left, was sharp and irritable.

There was an answering murmur, presumably from the footman, and an instant later the doors opened wider, and a short, thickset man, carrying an ivory-tipped walking stick, crossed the hall. He was certainly old, she thought, but there was no softening of the years in his harsh face with the still plentiful grey hair and the cold, bright eyes under beetling grey brows.

'Mr Royston?' she ventured as he continued to stare at her.

'I don't see anyone without an appointment,' he barked.

Not a man who would give casually to charity, whatever his philanthropic intentions. She took a slightly longer breath than usual and said, 'I'm here to apply for the position, sir.'

'What position? Have we need of more staff?'

The question was rhetorical, the footman having melted discreetly away.

'Assistant curator,' Tansy supplied helpfully.

'That vacancy hasn't yet been advertised. How did you — '

'Your assistant curator died last month of gastric fever,' Tansy said boldly. 'I read about it in the newspaper and I've not heard of anyone else being appointed yet to replace him.'

'Quite right. Nobody has. What makes you think you are qualified for the post?'

Tansy took another long breath and answered steadily. 'I live in Chelsea within walking distance of the museum. I'm a single lady of independent means and would work more for the interest of the employment for I do have a great liking for antiques.'

'So you'd work for nothing?' he interrupted.

'Only a fool works for nothing,' Tansy said shortly. 'I'd expect fair recompense for a fair day's work. The truth is that I don't want to spend the rest of my life plucking weeds from my garden or attending vicarage tea parties,' she said shortly.

'If you need occupation,' he said, 'then take up embroidery.'

'I need more to occupy my mind than the sorting of silks!'

'Liking antiques is not the same as knowing anything about them,' he said.

'That's true and it's also true that I've never been formally trained,' she retorted 'but I'm a quick learner and I've always loved being among beautiful and historic objects.'

'Good point, Miss Clark!' He nodded, unexpected approval edging the curtness of his tone.

'A true one,' Tansy said.

For a moment more the cold, bright eyes

were fixed on her. Then he said, 'Come with me!'

He had turned and was making his way towards the room on the left before she took one step forward. This, she mused, was a man who pleased himself at all times, a man whose deeds of philanthropy had very little to do with warm-hearted charity.

The room was a huge one, running from back to front of the house. Flat against the walls at each side of both sets of long windows were fastened iron grids which, she guessed, would be pulled across and securely locked when dusk fell. The chamber itself was austere with a floor of polished wood, its walls painted a light brown against which a variety of glass-fronted cabinets stood with, at intervals, a long sofa placed between them.

'Walk round slowly,' Mr Royston said, turning abruptly, 'and tell me which object most takes your fancy, which one strikes you as being most ancient. Take your time.'

Tansy hesitated and then began a slow perambulation about the room, pausing at each cabinet to look at the objects within.

Geoffrey's particular interest had been pottery and they had spent many happy hours looking at the exhibits in the local museums, she eager to share in her fiancé's hobby.

'Ming, sixth dynasty. You can tell by the brushstrokes. No, that vase is a fake, Tansy. The colour is too thickly applied and that crack too regular to be authentic.'

She had at least learned something, she thought, and wished as she moved slowly round the large room with its cabinets that she could turn to Mr Royston, whose keen eyes followed her slow progress, and inform him that the elaborately chased samovar within had actually come from Manchester or Birmingham! It was obvious, however, that a man like Royston would have every purchase authenticated twice over.

'This looks very old,' she said at last, pointing to a large buckle of reddish-gold that lay on black velvet behind the glass. 'If I touch things I get a better picture of their age.'

'Not the most ancient artefact I have,' he told her, drawing nearer, 'but the first thing I ever excavated when I was a boy. A buckle from the cloak of a Roman soldier from the first century. It has little monetary value — the legions were in the habit of dropping their rubbish whenever they moved their quarters, but it was my first authentic find and so has a certain sentimental value for me. You will pardon an old man's vagaries?'

Anything less sentimental than his keen,

44

cold, bright glance she had yet to see.

Inclining her head with what she hoped was sufficient graciousness she moved on to the next cabinet which had no glass through which one might view the treasure within but was delicately carved of sandalwood which gave off its musky perfume.

'I am wondering,' she ventured, 'why someone would have a cabinet and not display what was in it — or is the cabinet itself the artefact?'

'I had it specially made,' Mr Royston replied. 'Not all treasures are for the public gaze and this one awaits its occupant. You know very little about antiques, Miss Clark, but you have a questioning eye. No qualifications, no references, but you present yourself boldly at my house. Initiative is something I have long admired! I can offer you two guineas a week and a fortnight's trial in my museum. You may start tomorrow morning — five days a week from ten in the morning to three in the afternoon. After summer the light fades too swiftly for the exhibits to be seen properly or appreciated. Wait here!'

He turned and went out, tapping his stick rapidly on the floor. Tansy had the feeling that he used it for emphasis rather than for aid. Certainly he was a formidable character!

This room itself had the atmosphere of a museum to which hardly anybody ever came. She guessed that a man like Carl Royston would have few if any intimate friends.

The tapping of the stick roused her from speculation as Carl Royston came back into the room, a sealed letter in his hand.

'This letter authorizes you to work as assistant curator in my Chelsea museum for a probationary period of two weeks,' he said, handing it to her. 'The head curator is William Benson. He will very likely set you at once to brewing tea and doing a little light dusting.'

His tone was deliberately provocative but she smiled sweetly without comment as she took the missive with its elegantly written address.

'Thank you, Mr Royston,' she said.

'Good day to you, Miss Clark, and pray give my regards to your father.'

'You know Pa?' Her eyes widened slightly.

'Many years ago a young constable called Laurence Clark was part of a team investigating the theft of a collection of rare coins in which I took great pride. The coins were recovered with the minimum of fuss and bother. I have followed his progress from a distance with interest ever since. He had red hair too. You are a feminine version of him.'

'You should have told me that you remembered him, sir,' Tansy said.

'Oh, there's very little I ever forget,' he said, and bitterness weighed down the statement before he added, 'You need not imagine that I hand out employment to relatives of the police force on the basis of a distant and exceedingly slight acquaintance-ship. Unqualified though you are, you do seem to possess some common sense, which is why I have hired you. I hope you will enjoy working in the museum. Philips!'

The tall, thin footman appeared within seconds and she was shown out with rather more politeness than she had been admitted.

★   ★   ★

Some time later, she sat back in her chair and raised a questioning eyebrow at her father.

'What do you make of it, Pa? He obviously recalled you.'

'Though I played a very minor part in the investigation.'

He tapped the bowl of his pipe with his fingers and frowned slightly.

'Perhaps he too has suspicions about his assistant curator's death and hopes the mystery will be solved,' he said mildly.

'That's hardly likely!' Tansy protested. 'My

47

name has never appeared in any newspaper in connection with either of our previous cases!'

'Perhaps he wishes to return a good deed for the work the force did when his coins were recovered?'

'Pa, you've met Carl Royston! He's the kind of man who forgets about good deeds but returns bad ones with interest!' she exclaimed.

'A hard man of business,' he agreed.

'But he did found the museum for a charitable purpose.'

'Perhaps he hoped for a knighthood,' Laurence said cynically. 'Her Majesty, however, is not in the habit of handing out knighthoods willy-nilly, especially when the man in question makes a profit out of his philanthropy.'

'You think he too has suspicions about his assistant curator's death?'

'It's possible.'

'But he's rich enough to employ the best of private detectives,' she protested.

'He may have contemplated doing so and then you arrived on his doorstep most opportunely. Pass me that volume, will you? There is some information about him in there.'

She reached up and handed down the heavily bound book in which details of the eminent in society were listed.

'Let's see.' Her father's fingers riffled through the gold-edged pages. 'Here we are! Carl von Reuston, born in Vienna in 1800, English mother. Naturalized British subject, 1825. Philanthropist and art collector. Married Vashti Saig in 1848. Son Benjamin born in 1848. That's all.'

'Vashti is a beautiful name,' Tansy said.

A romantic name, she thought, that conjured up visions of gleaming royal robes and jewels glinting against black tresses.

'Vashti — ancient Persian queen,' her father said. 'She's in the Old Testament somewhere and I can't think where.'

'Book of Esther,' Tansy supplied.

'Ah! You take after your mother,' Laurence said. 'She had a bit of a religious bent too. Well, all this doesn't explain why two museum assistants died of the same complaint within a month of each other.'

'Have you heard from Frank?' Tansy enquired.

'Not yet. Sunday isn't the best day for gathering information. So you start work at the Royston Museum tomorrow?'

'At ten sharp!'

'Tansy, be careful.' He spoke with a sudden gravity.

'I'm hardly likely to be in much danger

showing the odd visitor round and doing a bit of dusting!' she protested.

'Just remember that two assistant curators have recently died,' he warned. 'Tread warily.'

'Case the joint,' supplied Finn, who had just entered with his customary uncanny knack of knowing when his employer was beginning to tire.

'That,' commented the said employer, 'is a horrible phrase!'

'American,' Finn said. 'Lots of new phrases coming over the Atlantic.'

'Which should have stayed where they were,' Laurence said. 'Are there any cabs about?'

'I'll walk across the park,' Tansy said, resolving to correct her urge to avoid the leafy paths that had sent her round by the road the previous evening.

She had said nothing to her father about the strong conviction that she had been followed. Laurence had always encouraged her independence but she knew that he fretted about her and resented at a deep level his own inability to protect her.

Now he said, 'Tansy, be careful.'

'I always am,' she answered lightly. 'Bye, Pa!'

It was time to lay the ghost of the memory of her engagement to Geoffrey. Until she did that it was impossible for her to move on emotionally and she wanted to, though she was by no means certain in which direction.

Outside the fogs of the previous day had finally evaporated into a cobweb of mist that hung over the hedges and bushes or swayed in long ribbons from the trees. Will-o'-the-wisp, she thought, and smiled at her own romantic fancy.

This being Sunday afternoon and already edging towards dusk, those who had come to enjoy the fresh air and the flower scents or to help their children sail paper boats on the round pond or bowl their hoops were preparing to leave, small boys being dragged protestingly from the water's edge, nurse-maids firmly tucking up their charges.

A sudden pricking in the vicinity of her heart reminded her of loss and expectations not fulfilled. Thirty-five was hardly ancient but most doctors advised having children earlier to mitigate the perils of giving birth which, even with modern improvements to health care, were still something to fear. Her own mother had been unable to bear more babes after Tansy's birth and the son who might have followed Laurence into the force had never materialized. Not that her father had ever regretted the fact openly but she was positive that he must have done so in his innermost heart.

'This,' she said aloud, so loudly in fact that a uniformed nursemaid settling her small charge nearby took fright, gripped the handles of the perambulator and hurried away. 'This is just plain stupid!'

She quickened her pace, reminding herself that these days thirty-five was no age at all, that she was healthy, independent, comfortably off and had plenty to occupy her mind already.

What she ought to be considering now was how to find out as much as possible about the Royston Museum without causing the head curator to become suspicious.

She would, as Finn had picturesquely phrased it, case the joint thoroughly, report back to Laurence any very odd circumstances that roused her suspicions and she hoped, find that the whole suspected activities of curators and their employers rested on no surer foundation than the coincidence of two men dying of the same illness.

So thinking, she came face to face with the lilac bush where Geoffrey had proposed, seeing the long feathery blooms browning and falling to seed, and hearing clearly her own name spoken aloud beyond the foliage.

'Tansy.'

Without pausing to consider, without

waiting to hear her name repeated or to catch sight of the speaker, Tansy fled past the bush, skippering from the path to the grass, not daring to look back, the now-rising mist wreathing her ankles and drifting slowly across the nearby water where a short time before children had been playing.

4

'Tansy, wait!'

For a moment she failed to recognize the voice and then, shame suceeding panic, she slowed, stopped and turned as Frank, hat in hand, came panting up.

'What the devil ails you?' he demanded. 'You took off like a rocket!'

'You scared me half to death,' she said crossly.

'Surely you knew my voice?'

'I was thinking about something else,' Tansy said, adding hastily lest he pose an awkward question, 'I have a job at the Royston Museum!'

'You've been hired? How on earth? You haven't the least qualification — '

'I learn fast and I have an eye for the ancient and beautiful,' Tansy said loftily.

'I thought you were going to collect for charity.'

'I was but it's obvious that Mr Royston doesn't give casually unless there's glory in it for him.'

'You've met Carl Royston? Word is that he's something of a recluse.'

'He's very brusque,' she said. 'Used to having his way in all things! I think he enjoys trying to intimidate people.'

'I take it that he didn't succeed with you,' Frank said drily.

'I think that was why he hired me.'

'Or perhaps he wanted you somewhere that makes it easier to keep an eye on you?'

'I hardly think that Carl Royston suddenly goes round murdering his assistant curators!' she expostulated, half laughing. 'Anyway, we don't know if there's any substance to Pa's suspicions yet.'

'You've seen your father?'

'I just left him.'

Briefly she recounted details of her visit.

'Vashti,' Frank said thoughtfully as she finished her account. 'That's a pretty name.'

'And certainly not a European one. Middle Eastern.'

'And Carl Royston was originally Carl von Reuston?'

'Not all people who are foreign-born are suspicious characters,' Tansy protested.

'Of course not! And since his original name et cetera is already published he clearly isn't masquerading as someone else,' Frank agreed.

'Finn would swear that all millionaires are thieves with servants,' Tansy said with a grin.

Now that her sudden fright had been allayed she found that she enjoyed strolling with Frank who, hat in hand, looked handsome if slightly ruffled after chasing after her.

They had almost reached the further gates, beyond which the pavement curved to the cab stand. There was a bench here, with ivy already thick with dark berries of autumn wreathing itself though the wooden struts.

'Shall we sit for a moment or two?' he enquired. 'My legs aren't as young as they were!'

'Don't be ridiculous!' Laughing, she seated herself and looked up at him. 'You can't be more than . . . forty-five?'

'Forty-three actually,' he said as he seated himself on the bench beside her. 'This is nice!'

'More peaceful now the children and nursemaids have gone and the moon is trying to escape into the sky,' Tansy said softly.

'And the breeze is gentle,' Frank said.

There was something perilously romantic in the air. Tansy drifted a fraction further away on the bench and said with conscious briskness, 'How about your day? Have you found out anything about the two men who died?'

'I went to the coroner's office,' he told her, his voice becoming businesslike. 'It's open on

Sundays only for emergencies but I know the clerk there quite well and he was good enough to check the records which are, of course, quite recent.'

'And?'

'Both men had complained of feeling poorly a week or so before they died,' he told her. 'Two separate doctors both diagnosed gastric fever in each of their patients. They independently advised similar treatment — clean water, a small dose of quinine and rest in a cool room.'

'Standard treatment?'

'Apparently carried out. Joseph Fanshaw died first. Brook Wilton was taken ill about three weeks later and died within the week.'

'Where did they live?'

'I got their addresses and went round to both places,' Frank told her.

'And?' Her voice was eager, her hands clasped tightly together.

'Fanshaw lived on the far side of Chelsea, which isn't too far from the Royston Museum where he worked. His landlady told me that he was a very quiet, respectable young man. Never had any visitors. Wilton lived over in Kensington. Same story — no family, no visitors, very polite and quiet. I've noted down their addresses for you but I doubt if you'll find out any more.'

He handed her a slip of paper on which the details were written.

'I could pretend to be a long-lost cousin I suppose?' she mused, stowing the paper in her purse.

'I think any long-lost relative would have turned up by now,' Frank objected.

'Did you see their rooms?'

'I must be losing my touch,' he said ruefully. 'The truth is that both landladies kept me chatting on the steps. You might have better luck but I'm beginning to think there's nothing else to find out.'

'When Pa gets a peculiar feeling,' Tansy said darkly, 'there's usually quite a lot to find out. His instinct for crime is as keen as ever it was.'

'Take care anyway,' he said soberly.

'I certainly will if you promise not to go hissing at me from behind bushes!' she retorted, rising as she spoke. 'I'd better get my cab, before Tilde weaves some fantastic tale to frighten Mrs Timothy into fits!'

'How is the fair Tilde?' he enquired, rising with her.

'Struck by the masculine charms of the butcher's boy,' Tansy informed him. 'She is on the verge of presenting him with an illustrious ancestry!'

They were moving towards the far gate but

she paused for an instant as the dying sun sent out a final glory of reddish gold that illumined the park for a few seconds before the purple of twilight crept over the scene again.

'Would you like to come back for a coffee or something stronger?' she heard herself say.

'I'd love to but I've an engagement. Another time?'

'Yes, of course.'

Odd, she thought as they strolled on, that she now felt obliged to issue a more formal invitation for a coffee when, for several years, he had been in the habit of calling casually.

She was glad she hadn't mentioned her sensation of being followed before, or volunteered any explanation as to why she had panicked and fled when she had heard her name spoken from behind the lilac bush. The uneasy thought struck her that he had finally accepted that her heart was still bound to Geoffrey and had begun to back off very gradually.

'This job you've taken,' he said abruptly, signalling to a waiting cab as they went through the gates.

'Yes?' Tansy looked at him.

'I don't think the two deaths were more than coincidental,' Frank said, 'but you will take care?'

'I promise,' she assured him. 'Anyway, I've often thought it might be interesting to work in a museum.'

He hesitated for an instant, then took her arm, turned her swiftly about to face him, bent his head and kissed her, not on the cheek where he usually bestowed a salute but on the lips, a caress that had in it something that promised more than the meeting of lips but was so soon over that he had called good night and was striding away before she could get her breath back.

Climbing into the cab, giving her address and resolving to be driven right up to the gate this time, she decided shakily that a job in a museum might settle her mind and prevent the stirrings of an unwanted desire.

★ ★ ★

The next morning, wearing the same rather drab outfit in which she had bearded Carl Royston in his mansion, she set off for the museum which, despite its closeness to her home, she had never visited — partly because since Geoffrey's death visits to such establishments reminded her too bleakly of what she had lost but partly also because Geoffrey had never troubled to take her round the place.

'Very dull,' had been his opinion. 'Hardly

anything worth collecting privately let alone displaying to the public there. Free entry is no excuse for a shabby display.'

Why, she scolded herself, must Geoffrey always come into her mind when her thoughts needed to be clear and concise? She dismissed his ghost and only realized as she reached the museum that she had begun to think of Frank instead!

Her job, she had decided, wasn't something to be confided to Mrs Timothy or Tilde. The latter would immediately leap to the conclusion that Tansy was in danger of being murdered and Mrs Timothy would decide that her employer was in such dire financial straits that she ought to offer to take a cut in her wages, which would be very bad indeed for her poor back.

Instead Tansy had murmured something vague about charity work and sallied forth briskly before too many questions could be asked.

It was a bright morning with the last lingerings of mist and dew to soften all the outlines. She had the letter from Carl Royston and a small notebook in which she intended to jot down her own impressions when opportunity allowed.

'Write it down,' her father had always advised. 'Even the best memory can play tricks sometimes. Anyway, written evidence always counts for more than word of mouth.'

She wondered as she walked along what she would have to write down in the book. Possibly nothing at all but working for a living made a change at least. She had just realized with a stab of self-disapproval that she was actually growing rather bored with her comfortable life when she arrived at the museum itself and, standing back for a moment to survey its façade, decided that her and Geoffrey's impression of it had been correct.

It stood back from the road with a notice too neat and small to attract much attention that announced it to be the Royston Museum. The front door was porticoed; the windows had grated shutters that could obviously be locked at night. The door was at least open and the curator had clearly been told to expect her since a thin, spare man who looked as if he ought to be among the exhibits, so dried up did he seem, rose from a small vestibule within the entrance hall and came to greet her in a stiff, unyielding manner that hinted at private resentment.

'I understand you have a letter of authorization for me?' he began.

His voice was flat and dull as if all the energy had been sucked out of it.

'From Mr Royston, yes.'

She handed him the letter and took her seat on the chair he silently indicated.

'You do not,' he commented after reading the letter slowly twice over, 'seem to be in very desperate need of employment, Miss Clark.'

'That's true, Mr Benson, but the idea of working in a museum among beautiful and ancient objects has always appealed to me,' she said brightly and with what she hoped sounded like conviction.

'Not many people come,' he said gloomily. 'They prefer the larger, more showy places. Not only museums but art galleries and theatres.'

He ended by pressing his hands together, having laid the letter aside, and grinding his palms as if he were crushing all other amusements out of existence.

'I understand,' Tansy said, hazarding a guess, 'that I shall be directly answerable to you.'

'To me, yes.'

He picked up the letter again and scanned it carefully.

'If I might know my duties?' she ventured.

'To guide the visitors round, give them information on the various exhibits — there is a book here that will help you. And keep the cases properly clean. Mr Fanshaw was sometimes a trifle careless about the dusting,' he said.

'I understand he died recently?'

'Yes. A most worthy young man but the end of life is always death. That is a precept I keep constantly in mind. This way, please!'

Though she strongly doubted whether there was a Mrs Benson, Tansy, trailing after him into the first room of exhibits, pitied the probably non-existent lady.

'Was Mr Fanshaw knowledgeable about the exhibits?' she enquired, looking at the figure of a Roman soldier who, standing on a plinth in his glass case, looked somewhat depressed.

'He did not encourage the visitors to linger,' Mr Benson replied. 'As you can see these are Roman coins, the remains of a sandal, armour which requires polishing at stated intervals, some beads which are reputed to have belonged to Boudicca, Queen of the Iceni, though I beg leave to question that assumption.'

On they went through rooms which did indeed hold some interesting items but their description in William Benson's monotonous voice rendered them dead as ashes.

'There is a small retiring room for ladies,' he said, opening a door and closing it just as quickly. 'You may avail yourself of the facilities. I have a small private office where I check the correspondence and across the road is a small café where one may obtain a cup of tea and a sandwich — convenient for myself since I can see who comes in and out here. I repair there at one sharp and return twenty minutes later. You may take your lunch as soon as I return. Since Mr Fanshaw's demise I have brought something with me to eat but tomorrow I shall resume my usual routine.'

'Portland stone!' Tansy said as they came into a corridor lined with shelves on which the jugs and vases stood in rows.

'Yes. They are somewhat heavy but still require dusting lightly.'

'And the staircase?' She nodded towards the stairs at the end of the corridor.

'Occasionally a new artefact is brought in or another requires expert cleaning or repair. That,' he added, 'does not occur very often and I would always be here to supervise any such activity.'

And that, thought Tansy, later that morning, seemed to be about the only exciting thing that ever happened in the Royston Museum! Having sorted through a pile of brochures and shown round two visitors, a couple of elderly ladies who obviously had half an hour to spare before luncheon, Tansy no longer wondered why Mr Benson seemed so melancholy — or had he been chosen to fit the tedium of his job?

'You may go for your luncheon now, Miss Clark,' the object of her speculations announced, emerging from his cubicle of an office. 'Pray take your time. Monday is one of our quieter days.'

She hadn't previously noticed the café opposite where the doorway lurked within a recess and the sign over it required urgent repainting, but the interior was clean and neat.

Spying a familiar figure seated in a discreet corner, Tansy crossed and sat down.

'Casing the joint, Finn?' she enquired sweetly.

'Getting a feel of the neighbourhood, more like,' he returned unabashed. 'And it's no use to frown at me, Miss Tansy. Following orders is all I'm doing. Pretty shabby part of Chelsea, don't you think?'

'Neglected,' she agreed, ordering eggs and toast and a pot of coffee from the waitress. 'Like a dusty cupboard full of stuff nobody wants — excepting yourself, of course,' he said.

'Why, Finn! I never realized you had an imagination before!' she exclaimed teasingly.

'It were imagination that got me into hot

66

water in the long departed days, Miss Tansy,' he informed her. 'Always fancied I could make one haul and retire on the proceeds, so to speak. If your pa hadn't taken an interest in me — but that's a blessing I never shall forget, Miss Tansy! What's the museum like inside?'

'So far fairly dull,' she admitted. 'There are some interesting things there but they're not displayed with much imagination at all and Mr William Benson is about as interesting as a sheet of blank paper. Are you here to guard me? I hope not because I really am capable of taking care of myself!'

'Never doubted it!' he assured her. 'Just for today your pa wanted a watch kept but it all seems as quiet as — '

'The grave,' she supplied.

'Not a subject for jest, miss,' Finn said. 'When I were a mite younger and more spry I thought of taking up grave-robbing as a bit of a change in my career, you might say — lots of folk like to have their jewels buried with them — but it were imagination let me down again. Somehow I never could fancy — well, you get the drift?'

'Only too clearly,' Tansy said severely, 'and if your imagination stopped you from turning to that trade then you ought to be glad you've got one. Now you get off to Pa and tell him that I'm perfectly fine with nothing of any interest to report.'

'I'll leave you to finish your eggs in peace,' he agreed with some reluctance. 'No point in calling attention to the fact you have friends.'

'Does that mean Frank will be taking over guard duty later?' she enquired.

'Not as I know, miss. Haven't seen Mr Cartwright today,' he said.

'Oh. Well, tell Pa I'm fine and I don't need a chaperon,' she said brightly.

Had Frank taken offence at the way she had responded to his kiss? Or rather not responded? It wasn't like him to take umbrage but then he had never kissed her on the mouth before. She frowned slightly and tried, not altogether successfully, to dismiss the little scene from her mind.

By three she had committed to memory the spiel with which she would inform visitors about the objects on display. However, as no more visitors arrived she studied the various pamphlets in peace and just before 3.30 was led round the building in order to witness the careful checking of the display cabinets and the drawing and locking of the grilles.

'I think I may say that my report to Mr Royston will be cautiously favourable,' Mr Benson said, ushering her through the front door before he locked it.

'Cautiously,' she thought, was hardly enthusiastic but then one would be foolish to expect something resembling enthusiasm from the solemn, dried-up figure who now shook hands with her and turned, presumably, in the direction of his own lodgings.

As he walked away Tansy reminded herself that she had no idea of his address. Had he a home near either of the two men who had died? It was something worth finding out when the chance came.

Meanwhile she walked briskly across the street, passing several people busy with mid-afternoon shopping. One or two turned to glance after her despite her simple, soberly coloured clothes.

Probably, she thought wryly, because it's obvious that a tall, gawky creature with red hair must be a spinster forced to earn her living as a governess or superior housemaid.

She wondered idly what would happen if she mounted one of the nearby blocks of wood on which the shoe shiners were inviting passers-by to place their feet and announced she was working in a museum full of the most unusual and exciting objects and everybody ought to rush along and view them immediately. Quite apart from the fact that the place was closed for the day, any visitors would be so disillusioned by the contents of the museum that they would probably rend her limb from limb.

That thought made her laugh out loud and walk on more cheerfully, unaware that several in the passing crowd had paused at the joyous sound and turned to look after the tall, slender woman with the wealth of red hair tucked behind her bonnet.

She had half expected Finn or Frank to meet her along the way now that her first day was done but there had been no sign of either. Finn she had warned away but she couldn't help a stab of disappointment from hurting her when she arrived at her gate without even a glimpse of the fair-haired journalist.

'There you are, miss!' Tilde cried, opening the front door as she saw her mistress coming up the short path. 'You must be worn out!'

'Hardly!' Tansy said, amused. 'There was very little to do.'

'Charity work can be a heavy burden,' Mrs Timothy added, coming through from the kitchen. 'Many's the time I've considered taking up good works but my back has always reminded me that some burdens would be too heavy for me to bear! I'll put the kettle on.'

'Did anyone call?' Tansy asked casually

over her shoulder as she began to mount the stairs.

'Not a single solitary soul,' Tilde said.

With which answer she had to be content.

5

It was the next day when, during the short luncheon break permitted, Tansy sat in the café opposite the museum eating a roll with ham and drinking a cup of coffee and, chancing to glance up from her window seat, saw a familiar figure approaching.

For an instant she had a leap of pleasure somewhere inside her but then the leap ended in a miserable sprawl. Frank, walking past and clearly in no particular hurry, looked in her direction and lifted his left arm in a casual salute. His other arm, she noted, was around the shoulders of a very pretty dark-haired young lady who wore a most fetching bonnet and an attractive pink velvet spencer. They went on together without pausing, leaving Tansy with a mouthful of half-chewed ham and the start of a friendly smile frozen on her face.

Of course Frank had other women, she scolded herself. One could hardly expect a man in his forties to be a virgin still! But his companion had obviously been a respectable young woman, hair neatly curled, heels low, no sign of feather boa or tinkling gold bracelets. In any case, such women as she obviously was not generally emerged after dark.

Frank, she reflected gloomily, had accepted his congé at last. The thought did not give her the satisfaction she expected. A friendship based on the occasional investigation seemed a poor substitute for shared intimacy. She pushed her coffee aside, paid the bill and crossed to the museum again with a heavy heart.

'Miss Clark, a person came with a note for you,' Mr Benson said. His tone was frigid.

'Oh? Tansy looked at him.

'It somewhat detracts from the dignity of the museum when notes are delivered to employees working a probationary period by other ... persons,' he said stonily, his hesitation before the word clearly registering his disapproval as he handed her the sealed paper.

'Thank you, Mr Benson,' Tansy said meekly, slitting the paper open and reading the brief contents.

Tansy girl,
Finn is bringing this to the museum. He tells me all seems well with you. Come and see your poor old dad this evening if you're not too tired.

Frank came over last night and will be eating here again this evening.

Tansy promptly decided that she would enjoy Mrs Timothy's cooking, which was not as good as Finn's since he favoured more exotic dishes but was always hearty and tasty.

'After the excitement of this job,' she informed the depressed-looking Roman in his glass case, 'I shall treat myself to a quiet evening at home!'

'Is there a visitor here?' The curator had hurried in.

'I was talking to Antonio here,' Tansy said brightly.

'The figure,' said Mr Benson, eyeing her with some alarm, 'is not real, Miss Clark. No entire Roman has ever been excavated to my knowledge except for skeletons since the Romans did not as a rule follow the Egyptian practice of embalming.'

'And I suppose his name wasn't Antonio,' she said.

'Miss Clark, wooden models with wax heads are never given names,' he said.

'Hush!' Tansy couldn't resist cautioning. 'He might hear you and then his feelings would be injured!'

'I see you have a sense of humour,' Mr Benson said, his expression troubled. 'Well, as long as it doesn't interfere with your duties I see no real harm in it. But pray don't allow any of our visitors to overhear you in such eccentric flights of fancy.'

He bestowed upon her what he evidently took to be a smile and went back to his office.

Tansy got on with the polishing and dusting. If she had charge here, she fantasized, she'd bring in more figures clad in reproduction garments — females and children — and have them all grouped in some scene, perhaps round a low table eating, or dancing. That would give some idea of an age gone past. And from all but the most delicate and rare objects of which there were few, she would remove the glass cases and let people whenever possible touch what had once hung about the neck of some Syrian beauty or adorned the breastplate of a legionnaire.

At least she had a sense of humour, she thought somewhat dismally. The truth was that she was feeling very much out of humour at that moment. For some reason the image of Frank Cartwright with his arm around the shoulders of a pretty brunette in pink rankled. It was quite ridiculous and she was ashamed of her childish reaction.

'And you needn't look so sad for me,' she told 'Antonio' crossly. 'I am actually a most happy person!'

Deep down she wondered suddenly if that was really true. A general feeling of contentment wasn't happiness. True happiness, she thought, only became apparent when it was on the verge of disappearing.

She grimaced at the trend of her thoughts and moved on into the next room, where the glass cases waited to be polished.

The afternoon half over and her museum work, which was hardly challenging, over for the day, Tansy reminded herself that she was not going to dine at her father's house, made her way to the nearest small park, bought a glass of lemonade from a passing vendor and settled herself in tolerable comfort on a bench where she sipped her drink and contemplated her next move.

In her purse she had slipped the paper on which Frank had written the addresses of the two young men who had died. He had been unable to gain entrance, she recalled. Maybe she would have better luck.

Having finished her lemonade she emerged into the street and took a cab to the first of the names and addresses on the paper. This was Brook Wilton, who had lodged in Kensington near to the museum where he had worked, a museum she knew quite well and had sometimes visited with Geoffrey.

A roadsweeper acknowledged her friendly afternoon greeting with a smile and a shake of the head.

'Getting cooler, miss, with the days drawing in,' he remarked.

'Yes indeed!' Tansy paused to say. 'And the days bring the leaves down as they fade.'

'They will do it, miss,' he said, gloomily surveying his half-filled cart. 'Even now a few are making to flutter out!'

He scowled at the few leaves eddying within the cart as a breeze reached them.

Like evidence, Tansy thought suddenly as she smiled politely and walked on.

Facts that didn't fit; odd unrelated incidents that ought to fit in somewhere and refused to oblige!

She had reached the house she wanted and she paused to survey its façade with the delicate fanlight above the door.

Somehow she had briefly pictured the lodging house as being tucked down a side street in a more modest part of the neighbourhood. Apparently assistant curators were rather better paid than she had imagined, certainly better paid than she herself now was. On the other hand he might have possessed impressive credentials.

She rang the bell and after a moment the

door was opened by a maidservant in a neat dark dress.

'Is your mistress in?' Tansy enquired.

'One moment and I'll see. What name please?'

'Tessa Cartwright,' Tansy said, the pseudonym jumping into her mind.

'One moment, miss.'

The maid vanished, returned almost immediately and beckoned her into a pleasantly furnished hall with a short staircase leading up to what, as she followed the other, turned out to be a large drawing room furnished comfortably, with a figure seated bolt upright on a straight-backed chair.

'Miss Cartwright? Forgive me if I don't rise,' the elderly woman said. 'On some days I am quite mobile but rheumatism is a sad affair, striking most often when the wind changes. What is your business with me?'

'I understand you rent out rooms,' Tansy began.

'Only to gentlemen. This is a gentleman's establishment.'

'Oh,' Tansy said brightly. 'This enquiry is not on my own behalf but on my brother's. He has just completed his law studies and requires a respectable place — '

'The Inns of Court are surely more

78

suitable. My pardon, I ought to have introduced myself. Old age damages one's manners, I fear. I speak with some authority as my late father was a barrister and I grew up hearing all about the training of lawyers. I am Mary Calcot.'

Which explained her ladylike demeanour. Tansy had heard her father speak years before of the acute intelligence and debating skills of Mr Calcot. Obviously he had left this handsome house to his spinster daughter and she was now renting it to other respectable young men who were just embarking on a career.

'I wondered,' she said aloud, 'if there was a room available — for my brother?'

'Whose name is?'

'Timothy,' Tansy said. 'He is very quiet and gentlemanly. I can vouch for that.'

'Then he will not progress very far in the legal profession,' the old lady said briskly.

'But if there is a room . . . ?'

'I would require him to come in person,' Miss Calcot said. 'There was a man here the other day making enquiries. Unfortunately he was a journalist, the most vulgar of professions. I told Susan not to admit him. My lodger, Mr Wilton, died recently and his death was reported in the newspaper — quite unnecessary as he had no living relatives

— so I dare say this man read it there or even wrote the piece. I cannot recollect the name he gave.' She wrinkled her brow but to Tansy's relief obviously failed to remember. Instead she said in a businesslike tone, 'Tell your brother to enquire personally. I cannot however hope to guarantee that the room will remain vacant. Does he have red hair?'

'Who?' Tansy said, confused.

'Your brother, Miss Cartwright.'

'Fair hair,' Tansy said.

'I am relieved to hear it. Red hair in a female is unfortunate. In a man it is quite reprehensible,' Miss Calcot said severely. 'Mr Wilton had dark hair and eyes and was a very quiet and respectful young man. His death was really rather sad. Tell your brother to come and apply to me. Good afternoon.'

The brother she had invented wouldn't have fitted into the house at all, Tansy thought as she politely took her leave. Timothy was blond and good-looking and enjoyed the company of pretty ladies in pink. Rather like Frank, she thought irritably, hailing a cab and directing it to her own home.

She was tired and disheartened and decided she probably needed a tonic.

The temptation to go and dine at her father's house anyway was lessened by a headache, a rare occurrence in her life, which attacked her shortly after she arrived home. She took the lightest of suppers and went early to bed.

★ ★ ★

The next morning she greeted Mr Benson and went through to the room where the Roman brooded.

'You and me both, Antonio!' she said, wondering as she began the regular round of dusting why she had spent the previous evening eating toasted cheese and apple crumble in solitary splendour when she might have been out enjoying the cut and thrust of the conversation between Frank and her father. She consoled herself somewhat with the recollection that she had at least got inside one of the lodging houses and later that day planned to go to the house where Joseph Fanshaw had lived.

The day didn't drag as much as others had done. A party of foreign visitors arrived and she was certain her stock had risen in Mr Benson's estimation since she was able to converse with them in tolerably correct French.

After the visitors had gone, the curator had checked the exhibits as if, Tansy thought with a spurt of amusement, he feared one of the foreigners might have made off with an artefact tucked under his arm.

The late Joseph Fanshaw had worked at this very museum and his address was a mere twenty minutes' walk away. The afternoon was brisk and cool and she made her way to the address with little difficulty though it lay at the opposite end of Chelsea from her own dwelling and at some distance from the river.

This time she tried a slightly different approach, noting that a neat notice was fixed to a ground floor window, advertising a room for rent.

The woman who answered her ring at the bell was obviously the landlady herself, having a decided resemblance to the Wife of Bath, even down to the gap between her front teeth.

'Miss Clark!'

Being recognized caught Tansy off guard. She heard herself stammering, 'How did you know?'

'Why, Miss Clark, when your dear mother was alive and I was just walking out with my late husband — may God bless his soul which is a generous thought in me for he surely never gave me a moment's peace when he was alive! When we were walking out, my parents owning this very house where you and I both stand now, your dear mother used to come round collecting for her charities and you were often with her. A lovely little girl with curly red hair and the look of an angel! You've grown into a fine young lady.'

'Well, thank you.' Tansy hastily regained her self-possession and smiled sweetly.

'And are you collecting for one of your charities now?' the woman enquired.

Since she hadn't volunteered her name, Tansy could only guess that the pleasant elderly woman assumed she recalled it from her early childhood.

'Actually,' she said brightly, 'I'm helping out at the Royston Museum until a new assistant curator is appointed.'

'Why, Miss Tansy, the last one lodged here with me!' the other cried. 'A very quiet young gentleman but very well qualified. Seemed quite healthy too though he'd no family, poor soul! Worked his own way through the university, he told me — not that he talked much at all. I'd've called him a bit of a dark horse but he was that respectable! He died, you know — right here in my house. Gastric fever! Such a shock and I'm sure it had nothing to do with my cooking for your dear mother always did me the honour of eating a slice of my sponge cake when she called and it agreed with her wonderfully. 'Mrs Owen,' she used to say, 'I'm sure that nobody can make a sponge as light as you can!' '

At least she had now discovered that her name was Mrs Owen, Tansy thought on a surge of relief, as she said aloud, 'I believe I read about the death of the assistant curator in the newspaper.'

'And your father, being retired police — and that was a sad thing to happen to a fine man! — he'd naturally be interested in any deaths,' Mrs Owen said. 'I had one of those nasty reporter fellows round asking questions the other day — very nice-looking, but I know his sort on account of having experience of the type with my late husband — and I wouldn't let him in to satisfy his curiosity!' Frank must be losing his touch, Tansy thought. Before she could frame another remark Mrs Own said, 'But it's very rude of me to keep you standing here. Won't you come in for a spell?'

'Does that mean you've baked a sponge cake?' Tansy asked.

'Not a sponge cake no, but some biscuits that fairly melt in the mouth, and a nice cup of tea to go with them! What do you say?'

'It sounds delightful,' Tansy said gratefully.

'Come along in, do!' Mrs Owen pushed her front door wide, hastily removed the broom with which she had been sweeping the front step, and ushered Tansy into a small but very clean parlour — clean save for the photograph of a middle-aged man on the wall whose features were obscured by dust.

'My late husband,' Mrs Owen informed her, noting her visitor's glance. 'Led me a hard life and when he finally went — in drink, as you might guess — I vowed that his picture could hang there until the end of time but I'd never dust it! Sit yourself down, Miss Clark, and I'll bring in the tea and the biscuits.'

They were duly brought, the tea proving to be refreshing and the biscuits delicate. Tansy, reminding herself that she'd no plans for the evening — no plans for the weekend, come to that — settled herself to an hour of reminiscences.

'It was the name you know,' Mrs Owen was saying. 'Tansy is such a pretty name. Your dear mother told me you were named after a flower — a wild flower but none the worse off for all that. I promised myself that if I ever had a little girl I'd call her after a wild flower too, but there were never any children, my late husband not being inclined that way. Another biscuit?'

'No, honestly! I shall have no appetite for my dinner,' Tansy said, beginning to rise. 'I am sure Mr Fanshaw appreciated your cooking. Have you had many enquiries since?'

'One or two but nobody I'd fancy sleeping under the same roof,' Mrs Owen said darkly. 'I don't suppose you'd like to see the room? Then if you chanced to know a suitable tenant you could recommend it to him?'

'I'd be happy to see it,' Tansy said, feeling positively overjoyed at the prospect. At least she would have stolen a march on Frank, whose journalistic standing prohibited him from viewing Mrs Owen's accommodation!

The room, a fair-sized one, was at the front of the upper storey and furnished neatly with a preponderance of tassels on the curtains and the bed neatly covered with a white quilt.

'He'd very few belongings, poor soul,' Mrs Owen said, looking round. 'I went to the funeral, you know. I understand the museum paid the expenses.'

'And he had no relatives at all who might've appreciated some personal memorial?'

'His clothes were sent to a charity,' Mrs Owen said dolefully. 'The museum took his books though they were kind enough to ask me if I wanted anything. He had no nice romantic stories, though, only books about dead things dug up in deserts. Not bedtime reading!'

Nothing here then to give her any hints as to the character of the man who had died here.

'I take very few lodgers,' Mrs Owen said, 'but I do my best to make them feel at home, and of course, being a Christian woman though not, I hope, a preachifying kind of person, I always slip a copy of the Good Book into a drawer — Pardon me! That'll be the fish!'

She went off to deal with the matter. Tansy moved to the chest of drawers and opened the top section, taking out the Bible that occupied the space in solitary splendour.

She opened it, or rather it fell open, at a page that must have been perused many times.

'The Book of Esther,' Tansy said aloud and stared at the name Vashti which, whenever it appeared, was ringed in red.

A moment more and she had thrust the Bible into her bag and was descending the stairs to bid the kindly Mrs Owen farewell.

6

Usually the weeks sped past on silver hooves but the four days she had worked at the Royston Museum had dragged on leaden feet. Tansy, realizing that Friday morning had at last arrived, heaved a sigh of relief and dusted vigorously, though only Antonio was around to approve her efforts.

The weekend loomed ahead, empty of engagements or appointments. She would go and see her father, she resolved, and let him know what little she had discovered. She hoped Mrs Owen wasn't aware of the theft of the Bible. Tansy herself had perused it closely, finding no other marks in its closely printed pages. If Mrs Owen did notice that it was missing, she would hopefully assume that Tansy had undergone a sudden conversion.

During the morning she showed round two ladies who had obviously taken a break from their shopping. One of them had on a pink cape — pink, Tansy decided crossly, was really a rather tedious colour.

What was becoming clear to her was that the museum, with its unvarying and unimaginative display of artefacts, held no clues regarding the deaths of the two assistant curators. It was possible, she reflected gloomily, that her father was simply bored and had fathomed a mystery where there was none. On the other hand, there were the red circles surrounding the name Vashti in the Bible she had purloined.

'Miss Clark, it's necessary for me to go out for half an hour,' Mr Benson said, coming through from his sanctum. 'We shall be closing soon but I have an appointment with my bank manager.'

It was an opportunity to be alone in the place without this dried-up little man popping in and out to supervise her. Tansy said, not too eagerly, 'Appointments in one's bank can never be exactly timed. Would you trust me to lock up? It would save you having to return here and if you are delayed I shall have to remain after hours since I cannot possibly leave the building unsecured.'

'You show a nice sense of responsibility, Miss Clark,' he said, allowing a faint note of approval to slide into his voice. 'Very well. Here are the keys. You may take them home with you since I have a spare set in my lodgings.'

'I'll make certain everything is secured,' she said gravely.

'And I will see you on Monday morning.

89

Thank you, Miss Clark.' He nodded towards her and, as if to show his approval further by humouring her, nodded also at the figure in the glass case.

To be alone in the museum was something of a relief. Tansy listened patiently as Mr Benson, coated and hatted, reiterated the exact instructions for locking up and smiled him off the premises.

To be on the safe side, lest he unexpectedly returned earlier than anticipated, she sorted through a pile of brochures which were clearly out of date, waited until 3.30 had chimed its single note from the clock on the wall and then drew the steel grids across, bolted them into place, locked the front door and walked through to lock the back door, which gave on to a large yard where presumably deliveries were meant to be dropped, though so far nothing at all had been delivered.

When she walked through to Mr Benson's small office with its large interior window, she was disappointed to find it already locked. None of the keys he had solemnly handed to her fitted the door and the window had been bolted on the inside.

She wandered back past Antonio, considered and dismissed the possibility of giving him a brochure to read but decided that if Mr

Benson unexpectedly returned he might regard it as a joke too far.

It was past four and the light outside was gentling already. Tansy wandered through the rooms with their glass cases and neatly ticketed rows of exhibits and decided irritably that she was bored. Ahead of her was the passage leading out of the room where the Portland stone was arrayed. She looked up at the short staircase.

She had mounted the stairs once or twice to fetch something that the curator needed but she had seen nothing but a low-ceilinged attic with shelves containing bits and pieces of broken glass and scraps of leather and other material and several packing cases denuded of their contents and spilling straw on to the bare boards.

It would do no harm to take a look she decided, and mounted the steps, the air becoming more dusty and stifling as she entered a space where windows were obviously never opened.

It was dispiriting to stand and look round at the jumble and the spilled straw.

More and more she began to feel a certain sympathy with Mr Benson, who must once have prided himself on obtaining the post of chief curator at the Royston Museum, never dreaming that having founded it, Carl

Royston would lose all interest in the project.

Why, she wondered, as a sudden spattering of rain tapped the windows, did Mr Benson place so much emphasis on locking up the place so securely? An overdeveloped sense of responsibility or was there something here that genuinely needed to be guarded? At least the rain, which had abruptly become a downpour, gave her an excuse for lingering here after hours should Mr Benson take it into his head to return. She had fortuitously neglected to bring her umbrella.

In a far corner of the attic she spotted a couple of opened parasols and, debating with herself whether or not to borrow one, moved towards them, lifting them up gingerly and promptly sneezing violently as a shower of dust assailed her.

They would afford no protection at all, she judged, one having its spokes bent crazily and the other having a large rent in its faded silk. She began to replace them and realized as she bent that they had concealed a cupboard door with no apparent means of opening it visible in the shape of handle or keyhole.

It was probably only a wall panel, she decided, giving its dusty wooden surface a sharp bang with her fist.

Accidents sometimes worked to one's advantage. The panel slid somewhat jerkily aside, thus revealing a cavity within in which stood a cardboard box.

Tansy knelt down and tugged out the box, which proved unexpectedly heavy. Its top was closed tight but the seals were cracking and it took only a few moments for her to prise them loose and slide out the contents.

Crumpled brown paper and straw came out together with a small, narrow, wooden figure crudely shaped into a female form with the face left blank and a wooden robe covering the hands, legs and feet or, to be more accurate, she decided, substituting for them.

It didn't even look particularly old, she thought, standing it upright and staring at it. It was no more than eighteen inches high and it conveyed nothing to her at all. Yet it had been stored here in a secret compartment for what, judging by the state of the cardboard box, must have been some considerable time.

It was the work of only a few minutes for her to replace the straw and brown paper in the cardboard box, roughly resecure the seals and put it back in the cavity, the wooden panel sliding back with a small click. The figure she would take to her father, she resolved, looking around the cluttered space and finally dragging out a faded carpet-bag from under a pile of rusty and stained material, which might once have been intended for curtains, and putting the wooden figure inside.

It was twenty minutes walk to her house but the rain was still heavy, bouncing spitefully up from the cobbles, and she was uneasy lest the figure of the curator on his way to check up should suddenly hover forth through the pelting water.

A cab drew up and she hailed it thankfully, finding herself at her own front door in record time and tipping him handsomely.

'Oh, miss, you are wet!' Tilde said as she opened the front door. 'You never took your umbrella either!'

'I got a cab most of the way,' Tansy said briskly. 'Has anyone called?'

Tilde shook her curly head.

'Not a soul, miss,' she affirmed. 'What, asks Mrs Timothy, would you be fancying for your meal?'

'I shall bathe and change and take a cab over to my father's,' Tansy said, making her way up the stairs with the carpet-bag bumping against her knees.

'Oh yes, miss!' Tilde approved. 'It's a few days since you went there. No trouble?'

'None at all but it's nice of you to fret about it,' Tansy said and went on up.

There was no point in wasting time in any

further inspection of the carving. She removed it from the carpet-bag, which showed alarming signs of coming apart at the seams, and slipped it into a large waterproof bag of her own, stripped off her damp clothes and went through to the bathroom where she was pleased to find the water hot and the towels, fluffily white.

By the time she had changed into a more attractive skirt and jacket of soft blue and tamed her waterfall of red hair into a snood she felt refreshed and eager to display her find to Laurence and Finn and whoever else might be there.

The rain had spent itself and she could smell the damp scent of the dying lilacs as she made her way to the cab-stand.

Arriving at Laurence's she was greeted unexpectedly by Frank, who called something to Finn, who was obviously in the large kitchen where he made his culinary experiments.

'Have you taken up residence here?' Tansy enquired as he held open the door for her.

'Not quite!' He gave her his disarmingly boyish grin. 'I've been going through old newspaper cuttings trying to get some detail on Carl Royston but there's nothing there that contradicts what we already know.'

'Miss Tansy!' Finn poked his head out of

the kitchen door and beamed at her. 'We was getting a mite agitated when you didn't come over and you'd given me particular instructions not to keep an eye on you though it went against my natural instincts, so to speak, to leave you quite unprotected — '

'Nonsense, Finn!' Tansy said briskly. 'I'm not in the slightest danger in the Royston Museum. I do have some information of a kind though but I don't know how far it's relevant.'

'Tansy, is that you? Come up and tell me where the devil you've been all week!' Laurence's voice floated down from above.

'Coming, Pa!'

She made her way up the stairs, carrying the waterproof bag which was distinctly heavy.

Laurence, having wheeled himself to the landing, noticed it at once.

'Ah! You've taken up larceny and burglary in your spare time!' he said genially.

'There's plenty of that at the museum,' she informed him. 'I mean spare time. We get a mere trickle of visitors and the exhibits themselves are most dreadfully dull.'

'Then what's that? No, wait until we've eaten. Finn won't thank us if we don't do justice to his beef stew and dumplings.'

'And plenty to go round!' Finn trumpeted,

coming up the stairs. 'You know I've a notion I might be like one of them spiritual people what gets dreams and visions.'

'Good Lord!' Frank, bringing up the rear, exclaimed in amused astonishment.

'I got to feeling that the weather looking like it might rain, thereby cooling the earth, a nice piece of stewing steak would go well with the vegetables in a casserole — '

'Which we see before us!' Laurence declared.

'And as I was choosing the cut,' Finn was continuing, placing the casserole on the table, 'it entered my head as how I'd best buy extra for I felt in my bones that you'd be here tonight, Miss Tansy!'

'If I were you,' Frank said, as they took their places at the table, 'I'd stick to cooking. Anyway, Tansy was almost bound to come this evening to give us any information she'd contrived to ferret out!'

'Did you ferret out anything yourself when you were in Chelsea the other day?' Tansy asked. She carefully avoided looking directly at Frank, who sat on her left, but fished a bit of carrot out of her dish and looked at that instead.

'Ah! I wondered when you'd mention that,' Frank said, seemingly unembarrassed by her remark. 'I actually thought of bringing Miss

Harris in to see you but then I decided it would be wiser to defer the pleasure.'

'Oh?' Tansy speared the piece of carrot neatly.

'Susan Harris works at the Kensington Museum,' Frank said. 'She deals with correspondence and filing orders and that kind of thing. She's only been working there for a couple of years but she found the work interesting and Brook Wilton, the other assistant curator who died, was very pleased and helpful to her whenever they happened to run into one another.'

It wouldn't be very difficult, Tansy thought, for a man to be pleasant to a girl with curly black hair dressed in pink!

'It so happened that during the week Wilton died she had taken time off to look after her aunt and since nobody had been officially appointed to take over during her absence she had quite a lot of work to catch up on when she returned. There was a note there addressed to her. She read it, was puzzled and alarmed and finally, not wanting to invite ridicule by going to the police, brought it to the newspaper office.'

'And?' Laurence nodded enquiringly.

'You know this already?' Tansy accused.

'If you'd cared to look in on your poor old father during the last couple of days you'd be privy to it too,' he retorted.

'To the note? What did it say?'

'The note's in the hands of the chief coroner, who is considering whether or not to have both bodies exhumed for more intensive examination.'

'For heaven's sake! What was in the note?' she demanded.

'I made a copy,' Frank told her. 'She affirms it is in Brook Wilton's handwriting and its content was certainly sufficient to arouse some suspicion in the minds of the authorities.'

'So what does it say?' Tansy demanded.

'That's my copy.' He handed it to her.

Dear Miss Harris,
This illness is coming upon me fast. It was the tea. I am certain it was the tea, but I have no proof.

'The actual handwriting was rather ragged but Miss Harris identified it as Brook Wilton's hand,' Frank told her. 'It was written in pencil and posted in the letter box almost opposite his lodgings. He sent it to her at the Kensington Museum but of course she didn't receive it until she returned from tending her aunt and by then both funerals were over. Anyway, there may be a further enquiry so it does look, sir, as if your suspicions were justified.'

'They very often are,' Laurence said mildly.

'And Tansy is carrying a suspiciously large waterproof bag,' Frank said, glancing at her.

'I was shown the bedrooms where the two men died,' Tansy said modestly.

'How did you contrive that?' Frank demanded. 'Those two battleaxes wouldn't allow me past the front door!'

'Because you belong to the nasty newspaper fraternity,' Tansy said. She supposed that Miss Susan Harris wore plainer clothes when she worked at the Kensington Museum but in any case pink was really quite a charming colour.

'So what happened?' Laurence asked, pushing his plate away and concentrating his full attention on her.

She told them, in the succinct manner her father approved of, about her two visits.

'And the Bible with the name Vashti ringed in red is on my bedside table at this moment,' she finished triumphantly.

'Why didn't you bring it with you?' he enquired.

'I forgot,' she said somewhat sheepishly.

'Tansy, it's always essential to preserve evidence carefully,' he said.

'I brought some more evidence with me,'

she protested, nodding towards the carpet-bag.

'Pudding first,' Finn said sternly. 'Chocolate truffles with rum butter. The beef suited you fine?'

'As usual the meal is excellent,' Laurence approved. 'You always contrive a lavish feat.'

'Well, I'm not paying for it,' Finn said cheerfully. 'I'll make the coffee!'

Coffee handed round, together with the truffles, Tansy shot an enquiring glance at Frank.

'Apart from helping Miss Harris start a new investigation going,' she asked, 'have you found out anything else?'

He shook his head.

'I, however,' Laurence said, demolishing a truffle and rinsing his fingers, 'have spent some hours in going through old newspaper files — I always knew it would be wise to hold on to anything of that nature I had! Finn can be relied upon to find a copy of anything I don't have on my shelves, usually in a second-hand bookshop.'

'Them second-hand bookstores are a cruel temptation to the reformed criminal,' Finn put in. There was a certain lingering trace of regret in his voice.

'What more did you find out?' Tansy asked.

'Carl von Reuston, father also a Carl,

mother British, name of Eliza Prudie. He was born at the turn of this century — March 27th, 1800. In Vienna.'

'An Aries then,' Finn said.

'A what?' Frank looked a question.

'Astrology,' Finn said. 'Always had a leaning towards it personally. Comes of being interested in so many things, I dare say. Arians are leaders, get-ahead-fast people who beat down the opposition.'

'That's a sweeping statement!' Tansy complained.

'Well, there's ascendants and mid-heavens and such to be studied,' Finn admitted, 'but I never did find the leisure time to go into all that.'

'Finn, you are a constant source of amazement to me!' Laurence declared. 'However, we'll forego further information on the somewhat dubious science of astrology and concentrate on the matter in hand. Carl von Reuston seems to have been devoted to his mother who died when he was about twenty-five. At all events, when his father died some ten years later, he applied for and obtained British nationality. The von Reustons were a wealthy family, deriving their money from various businesses in India and the Near East. Anyway, Carl von Reuston, having changed his name to Royston, came to

102

England in 1830 and settled here. He did, however, travel often in order to keep an eye on his various investments and business holdings, I suspect, and also to collect various antiques. In 1848 he married a Vashti Saig, daughter of an Ibn Hassan — Arab-Berber — and a French woman, name not recorded. She was 20 and he was 48.'

'He lost his head over her,' Finn intoned mournfully. 'It might well have happened to me but the thieving kept me fully occupied, so to speak.'

'She bore him a son, Benjamin, ten months after the ceremony — born and registered in London. Five years later Vashti left the child with his father and went off with another man. No further trace of her has been recorded.'

'And the son?' Tansy asked.

'A bit of a disappointment from the start from the little I've managed to gather,' Laurence said, nodding to the offer of a second coffee. 'Flunked school, was sent down from university, took no interest in fine arts but a great deal in chorus girls and racehorses. Regularly overspent his very ample allowance, had a blazing row with his father about five years ago and dropped out of sight. I imagine he probably settled, as far as it seems to have been in his nature to settle, abroad. Well, Tansy, that's all the information I've managed to glean. Now let's put ourselves out of our misery and open up that bag you've brought.'

'I don't know exactly what it is but it looks odd,' Tansy said, obediently moving to open the bag. 'I went up to the storeroom, which is full of rubbish and doesn't look in the least worth exploring . . .'

She briefly recounted how Mr Benson had left her to lock up.

'Certainly its being concealed in a wall cavity hints at this being more important or more valuable than it might appear,' Laurence said thoughtfully, 'but what exactly is it?'

'A kind of wooden figure, meant to be female, I think,' Tansy said doubtfully, pulling it clear of the bag.

By common consent they had moved away from the main dining table, Laurence wheeling himself near the brightest lamp.

'I wondered if it contained anything else,' Tansy volunteered, 'but I can't see any joins. It seems to be carved out of one solid piece of wood.'

'Is it old, do you reckon?' Frank asked.

'I didn't get the feeling it was old,' Tansy said hesitantly, 'but it's so thickly varnished it's impossible to tell.'

'The varnish would hide any joins,' Finn said, feeling the object with a professional air.

'It's quite heavy but it looks unfinished,' Tansy frowned.

'It's a casing for something,' Finn said, sounding professional.

'It doesn't rattle,' Tansy pointed out.

'Whatever's inside probably fits sung,' Finn said.

'So what do you think, Pa?'

'Does Mr Benson go up often to the storeroom?' he asked.

'Hardly ever. Only the once since I've worked there and that was only to show me the place from the door: there's a big yard at the back of the museum where deliveries are made but there don't appear to have been any new deliveries for ages.'

'Leave this thing with me three or four days and I'll have the casing off and the varnishing ready to be done again if it's needed,' Finn said, with the confidence of an ex-criminal.

'What do you say, Tansy?' her father asked. 'You can slip it back next week.'

'If I'm still working there.'

Her future prospects as assistant curator seemed decidedly shaky. On the other hand the crude figure with its thick coating of varnish was, in view of the hiding place where she'd found it, distinctly intriguing.

The figure was put back into the waterproof bag and Tansy glanced at the clock.

'Time I was getting back,' she said reluctantly. 'Tilde and Mrs Timothy are busy worrying about me as it is.'

'Why?' Frank asked.

'Oh, no particular reason,' she said lightly.

There was no point in alarming anyone with the story of her having been followed home, if indeed she really had been followed home. Not for the first time she chided herself for an over-active imagination.

'I'll see you home,' Frank said.

It was exactly what she'd been hoping he'd say. The girl in pink turned out to be simply a young woman worried about the last note from a friendly colleague. It was with a feeling of dismay therefore that she heard herself say briskly, 'There's absolutely no need, Frank. Just hoist me into the nearest passing cab and I'll see you after the weekend. Tuesday, Finn?'

'I reckon I'll have the casing off by Monday,' Finn said.

'Monday then,' Frank said, somewhat stiffly.

'Night, Pa. Finn, that was a lovely dinner. I hope there's something exciting in the wooden figure. See you Monday.'

She found herself moving in something of a fluster, putting on her cloak before Frank had the opportunity to hold it out, tying on her hat and grabbing her gloves as if somehow she found herself in a desperate hurry.

'It's stopped raining anyhow!' she said brightly as Frank hailed a passing cab.

'Indeed it has,' he said. 'Good night, Tansy.'

He put out his hand, touched her cheek with his forefinger and held the door as she mounted into the cab. As she seated herself he slammed the door, stood back to wave on the cabbie and in a moment was hidden by the curve of the road.

Tansy bit her lip, though whether in relief or vexation she couldn't tell.

The ride home was at any rate uneventful and by the time she reached her gate she felt calmer though she still scolded herself for feeling agitated when there was no cause for it at all. Possibly, she consoled herself, it had been a reaction after her time spent searching for clues at the museum, always with the uneasy apprehension that Mr Benson might come back to check up at any moment.

She went up the path and fitted her key into the lock, hearing as she entered the sounds of talk and laughter from the kitchen. It was a real blessing that Mrs Timothy and Tilde got along together so well, she reflected, but she must remember that Tilde was a young woman now who needed more in her life than housework and shopping and the company of an elderly housekeeper with a bad back.

'No need to disturb yourselves!' she called out as she relocked the front door. 'I'll see you in the morning.'

'Did you go out again, Miss Tansy?' Tilde asked, coming into the hall.

'Again? What do you mean by again?' Tansy asked puzzled.

'You came in an hour ago,' Tilde said.

'Of course I didn't. I went straight to Pa's house and spent the whole evening there.'

'You were going up the stairs,' Tilde insisted. 'Mrs Timothy and I heard a door close and I came out into the hall here. The lamp wasn't lit and it was very gloomy but there was some light coming from the kitchen fire and you were going up the stairs with your cloak on and the hood up.'

'You were dreaming it.'

'No, miss,' Tilde said firmly. 'I called up to ask if you wanted anything but you just shook your head and went on up. I thought it was a bit odd especially as you'd come through the verandah door at the back when you nearly always come through the front door. I went into the sitting room to damp down the fire and one of the glass doors wasn't quite latched. And you'd dropped one of your gloves on the way in, miss. Here it is!'

Tansy took her glove, one of a pair of kid ones she owned, and stared at Tilde in the half-light.

'If it wasn't you, Miss Tansy,' Tilde whispered, 'then who's upstairs now?'

7

Completely at a loss for a sensible reply, Tansy stared at her.

'I'll get Mrs Timothy,' Tilde said in a hurried whisper and, clearly believing that reinforcements were necessary, darted back into the kitchen.

Tansy remained in the darkened hall, her eyes fixed on the staircase. Tilde, she reminded herself, had a vivid imagination. Ever since Tansy had found her gloomily contemplating a romantic suicide in four feet of water, the girl had exasperated and amused with her strongly held conviction that her father had probably been a French nobleman and her mother one of the great courtesans, her proof being that she recalled her late mother talking of having lived once in Paris. But Tilde never told deliberate lies. Something had led her to believe that Tansy had come in earlier.

Mrs Timothy came out into the hall, a heavy saucepan in her hand, though Tansy was certain her bad back would prevent her from rushing upstairs to do battle with the intruder.

'This is a mystery,' she intoned now. 'I'm sure Tilde saw someone she took to be you, miss, for she came into the kitchen and said you'd gone upstairs and didn't want anything. She was so bold as to suggest you were in a sad humour for you never answered her but just shook your head which is, I venture to remark, most unlike your usual habit, Miss Tansy.'

'I'd best go up,' Tansy said, half inclined to wish she had a bad back too.

'Take this!' Mrs Timothy offered the saucepan.

'No need,' Tansy said, beginning to ascend the staircase slowly and silently.

Upstairs on the left above her long sitting-room was her bedroom with a small bathroom next to it. The bedroom and bathroom on the right had been intended by herself and Geoffrey as a room for the child they had hoped to have or, failing that, for overnight guests. Since neither child nor guests had put in an appearance she had given the rooms to Mrs Timothy, who occupied them in solitary state, while Tilde slept in the small room behind the kitchen.

It was seldom that Tansy ascended these stairs without recalling, albeit cloudily as the years had gone by, that she and Geoffrey had climbed the staircase together, armed with samples of wallpaper and small squares of material for the decoration of the house. Tonight her thoughts, however, were on the small pistol, hidden beneath her petticoats in the middle drawer of her bedside cabinet. Pa had taught her to shoot in the days before his accident and though she had guessed even back then that he would've given a great deal to have a son to instruct, she had delighted him with her quickness of eye and hand. After Geoffrey's death, when she had decided to live in the house they had planned together before his voyage to Jamaica, Laurence had given her a small but deadly silver-handled pistol.

'I know you are perfectly capable of taking care of yourself and I certainly don't want you here perpetually fussing over me,' he had told her, 'but single women living alone do run certain risks, my dear. There are burglars even in Chelsea.'

But if someone was hiding upstairs already waiting for her return she would have to hope he hadn't rummaged through the drawers and found the weapon first!

Her bedroom door was closed but a thin line of light showed beneath it. She drew a deep breath and flung the door wide.

The room was empty but the bedside lamp burned on the side table and the window was half open.

'Miss Tansy, are you all right?' Tilde was calling nervously from below.

'Perfectly! I think whoever was here has gone. Come upstairs!'

She crossed to the cabinet and opened the drawer where her neatly folded petticoats lay, rummaged for an instant and thankfully brought out her pistol, chancing to turn with it in her hand as Mrs Timothy lumbered in.

'Oh, Miss Tansy, dear!'

She flung up her arms while in the doorway behind, Tilde, now possessed of the saucepan, stood round-eyed.

'Sorry!' Tansy said swiftly, hastily hooking the pistol into her waistband where it drew Mrs Timothy's still-horrified gaze. 'There's nobody here now. Whoever came in clearly climbed out through the window ages ago. Look! You can see where the creeper is broken in places.'

She opened the casement wider and shone the bedside lamp on the trailing creeper.

Both approached and looked out fearfully. Fearful but not cowardly, Tansy reminded herself. Both of them had been willing to support her against an intruder.

She pulled the window closed again and

turned to face them.

'He may still be here,' Mrs Timothy said, very low.

'Hiding in a wardrobe,' Tilde contributed, quite unnecessarily in Tansy's opinion.

'Let's take a look!' she said briskly and opened the door of her own wardrobe, which proved to be full of hanging garments and nothing else.

'The bathroom!' Greatly daring, Tilde went in and came out again a moment later, declaring triumphantly it was empty.

'As is Mrs Timothy's,' Tansy said, having taken a quick look round. 'Your bedroom?'

'If a man is in my room,' Mrs Timothy said truculently, 'it was not by invitation!'

'Under the bed?' Tilde said helpfully. 'I read that a court gallant once hid under the bed of Mary, Queen of Scots, and was beheaded as a punishment.'

'If anyone is hiding under my bed,' Mrs Timothy said darkly, 'he'll pray for beheading by the time I've done with him! Tilde, your back is younger than mine and not subject to the misery I endure! Just kneel down and take a look, there's a dear girl!'

Tilde obeyed, stuck her curly head under the flounced hem of the counterpane and withdrew with the tidings there was nothing there.

'I think,' Tansy said firmly, 'that all the windows should be secured and the locks checked on the doors. Leave the French windows for me to see to. And I also think we could all do with a nice pot of tea.'

'Fancy you thinking the figure you saw on the stairs was Miss Tansy!' Mrs Timothy was marvelling as they went down the stairs.

'I wasn't expecting anyone else to be on the stairs,' Tilde excused herself.

Tansy stepped back into her bedroom and looked round.

Nothing, it seemed, was out of place.

The bedside lamp still burned and the creepers against the outside wall were bent and broken. Nothing else had apparently been touched.

She sat on the edge of the bed and leaned to open her glove drawer.

A solitary kid glove lay on top of the others, partner to the one Tilde had found.

Why only one glove? Why?

She took up the glove, holding it between her hands, sliding her fingers over the smooth kid.

'I presume it isn't bad manners to present a lady with a pair of gloves? I have been so long in the more uncivilized parts of the world that my knowledge of etiquette is somewhat rusty!'

Thus Geoffrey, his eyes smiling though his voice was solemn.

'I believe it is quite in order,' she had replied, feeling the colour mount into her face as he had taken her hand and drew on one of the gloves.

It had been her 22nd birthday and she had known him for almost a year. They had met accidentally when, on a wet afternoon, she had dived into a second-hand bookshop to browse among the untidily stacked volumes until the downpour ceased, and he had been studying an atlas with a faint smile on his lips that suggested he didn't altogether agree with its accuracy.

They had fallen easily into conversation and the rain dwindling, he had suggested they might both relish a pot of coffee at a nearby café.

Over the pot of coffee they had talked at first with constraint and then, feeling more at their ease, about books they had mutually enjoyed and the latest play and other trivial matters that escaped her memory now but were drawing them almost inexorably closer.

On her 22nd birthday, almost a year later, he had given her the gloves. Less than a year after that he had asked her to marry him.

Almost twelve years and Geoffrey had died of fever in far-off Jamaica and the gloves, hardly worn because of the memories they evoked, had outlived their giver.

There was no sense now in dreaming about the past. What mattered were facts. It was a precept her father had drummed into her.

'Not a bit of use thinking a man looks like a thief. If you haven't got evidence, then he is in the eyes of the law as honest as any man.'

Tansy put the glove back with its partner and went downstairs again, hearing Mrs Timothy and Tilde talking in the kitchen quietly. No need to ask if they'd checked and locked doors and windows! She was amused when she entered the sitting room that though, obedient to her instruction, Tilde had left the verandah doors ajar, she had fenced in the gap with two large chairs, one balanced atop the other, which would have crashed down had anyone tried to enter from outside.

She righted them and pushed the doors wider apart. Outside the tiles of the terrace, along which plants were ranged in pots, gleamed under the light of an emerging moon.

If the intruder had entered through the French windows then he couldn't have had the glove with him already. And entering, he would have had to unlock the doors which had been, as usual, bolted on the inside. That meant, she reasoned, that instead of making his entrance through the verandah doors he had actually climbed up, breaking some of the creeper on the way, and got in through her bedroom window which, in defiance of Mrs Timothy's oft repeated assertion that the night air brought disease and plague and all manner of unpleasant things, Tansy kept slightly ajar. So he had swarmed up the creeper and drainpipe, entered her room — no, Tilde had seen him (why did she assume it had been a 'him'?) going up the stairs.

The intruder had been on his way down the stairs, having abstracted the glove from her drawer, had heard Tilde coming out of the kitchen and had promptly turned and made as if he was mounting the staircase. He had waited then, come softly down the stairs again, unbolted the French windows and left them slightly ajar, dropping the glove he carried perhaps because some noise from the kitchen had alarmed him. But why steal one glove?

For a mad moment she played with the ridiculous idea that the butcher's boy had resolved upon capturing a love token and had mistaken her bedroom for Tilde's chamber.

There was no point in puzzling over the matter further. She stepped back, bolted the French windows and drew the long curtains across, replaced the chairs in their normal positions and went up to bed, calling a cheerful good night to Mrs Timothy and Tilde who, no doubt, would sit up a further hour discussing all the frightful things that might have happened.

★   ★   ★

There was the weekend to be got through before she started again at the museum on Monday morning. The next day was definitely cooler. September was racing into October. Tansy put on her gardening apron and gloves, tied her hair back with a scarf and was shovelling up leaves when Tilde came to announce there were visitors.

'Mr Frank and a young lady — ' She had just begun when Frank walked out on to the verandah, hat in hand, obviously disposed not to stand on ceremony.

'There you are!' he exclaimed. 'Come in and meet Miss Susan Harris! She's most interested in the investigation we have going!'

There was nothing for it but to pull off her gardening boots and apron and plod in slippers through to the hall, where the dark-haired young lady now dressed in blue stood politely waiting.

'Miss Harris is the young lady who brought

the note she received from Brook Wilton to the attention of the authorities,' Frank explained somewhat unnecessarily.

Polite handshakes were exchanged and Tilde, standing by the front door still, told to bring coffee and biscuits.

'I do hope you will pardon this intrusion,' Susan Harris said in a slightly breathless voice, 'but Mr Cartwright told me that other people were also puzzled by the deaths of Mr Wilton and a Mr Fanshaw.'

'Did you know Mr Joseph Fanshaw?' Tansy enquired, trying to slip the scarf off her head and immediately regretting it as her mane tumbled from its holdings and strayed wildly over her shoulders.

'I never heard the name.' The younger woman — at least ten years younger, Tansy reckoned — sank gracefully into a chair. 'I had heard of the Royston Museum but no correspondence from that establishment ever passed through my hands. I did however know Mr Wilton's handwriting though the note waiting on my desk was written evidently in a great hurry.'

'What kind of person was Brook Wilton?' Tansy asked.

'Quiet, seldom spoke much at all,' the girl said, frowning slightly as if she were conjuring him back into her mind. 'Very gentlemanly.

Once he was good enough to walk home with me after work when there were no cabs to be had anywhere and some rather rough-looking people on the street. I live with my mother who is a widow and she worries about me rather so it was good of Mr Wilton to escort me.'

It was clear she would have no lack of escorts should she choose, Tansy thought, finding a narrow black ribbon in her pocket and securing her hair back with that. She was slim, neat and distractingly pretty with a trick of slightly widening her eyes when she spoke that ought to have been irritating but was in fact rather attractive.

'Mr Wilton gave no hint at any time that he feared anyone?' Tansy asked.

'Not to me nor to anyone else as far as I'm aware,' Susan Harris said. 'As I told you he was very quiet, concentrated much on his work, seemed to have no confidants in the museum itself but of his private life I know nothing.'

'Do you know if there's to be an exhumation?' Tansy enquired of Frank.

'We won't know that for a few days at least,' he told her.

'Then we can only wait,' Tansy said.

'Mr Cartwright took me past the Royston Museum to see if any feature brought anything to mind, but nothing did,' Susan Harris said.

'Yes, I did notice you,' Tansy couldn't resist saying. 'You are one of the fortunate people who can wear pink.'

'Oh, but auburn-haired ladies can wear pink too!' the other said eagerly. 'Not a bright pink which would clash most dreadfully but a very pale pink to set off the stronger shade of one's hair. Do forgive me for making a personal remark but your own hair is the most wonderful shade of titian. I envy it greatly.'

She was either very sweet-natured or very clever, Tansy thought with a twinge of unwilling admiration.

Could she possibly have been the one who had entered last night? She was shorter than herself but slim and on the dark staircase her figure might've appeared slightly elongated.

If she could get Frank to herself for a few moments she could tell him of the previous night's alarm and upset, but Frank seemed quite happy to sit drinking coffee and munching a biscuit while he glanced between them as if, she thought crossly, he was making comparisons.

'I promised to take Miss Harris for lunch,' he said now. 'Would you like to join us?'

'Oh no, thank you,' Tansy said hastily. 'I

must get the garden sorted out before the bad weather starts, and later on I have some shopping to do.'

'In that case we'd best leave you to it,' Frank said. 'You'll eat at your father's on Monday evening?'

'Yes, I promised him.'

He had evidently and very wisely said nothing about the wooden figure that Finn was stripping of its varnish.

'It has been very nice to meet you,' Susan Harris said, rising politely. 'Mr Cartwright assures me you are one of the most sensible people he knows.'

That's me! Tansy thought wryly, shaking hands and escorting them to the door. Good, sane, sensible Tansy Clark, titian-haired and thirty-five years old.

Her own lunch was a scratch one after which she checked the notes in her purse and combed her hair neatly into a roll at the back of her head, told Tilde she would be at home all evening, and betook herself to the shops where after much thought and a little persuasion from the sales lady, she spent a considerable amount of money on a dress of thin wool with a pale pink bodice and a white skirt embroidered lightly in pink, a full-length coat of the same pale shade and a rather dashing pink bonnet with one of the new shallow crowns.

Happily, even when she reached home and tried on the outfit again before her bedroom mirror she was bound to admit that it suited her admirably.

It was a pity she had no engagement for the evening. She occupied it instead in going carefully through her possessions in the hope of finding that something else had been disturbed or taken.

She also, half sadly, half unwillingly, took out the little packet of letters that Geoffrey had written to her during their engagement and during the time before their intended marriage when he had been settling his late father's business affairs in Jamaica. His neat italic hand brought him back too vividly to mind for comfort and she tied them up again and laid them away.

Sunday meant church, a solitary luncheon and an afternoon, she decided, continuing to sort through her belongings. She paid scant attention to the sermon, however, and her own excellent lunch of baked ham with mashed potatoes and onion gravy lost some of its savour as she heard Tilde and Mrs Timothy chatting amiably together in the kitchen.

'Oh, I'm sure Miss Tansy will marry well one day,' Mrs Timothy was saying. 'She's an independent young lady though so she can afford to pick and choose.'

'If she doesn't take Mr Frank soon he may go off and marry someone else,' Tilde said with all the wisdom of her almost 21 years. 'I've seen it happen before. My own mother might have been splendidly wedded but she hovered and havered and in the end — She was too particular, Mrs Timothy, and that's the truth of it!'

Their voices dropped and Tansy looked gloomily at her almost cleared plate and wondered if some people started gobbling their food in middle age because it filled another emptiness deep inside them.

8

There was absolutely no sense in giving in to the rare despondency that had fallen upon her. She finished sorting out her wardrobe, reminding herself that she needed a new coat for the winter, the old one having seen better days, changed her new pink dress for a more practical grey outfit and pulled on a pair of walking boots.

'Exercise is the enemy of melancholy!' Laurence had once proclaimed though in what context she could no longer remember.

She spared a moment's regret for her father, who had been confined to a wheelchair for so long but still resisted any feelings of depression that must surely creep over him from time to time, pulled on a serviceable jacket, tied a scarf beneath her chin and called to Mrs Timothy and Tilde that she was going for a walk.

'It'll be dusk quite soon, Miss Tansy,' Tilde objected. 'The *crépuscule* as the French call it, or so Mama once told me. *Crépuscule* sounds rather Gothic and morbid, don't you think?'

'I shall try not to think of things like that,'

Tansy assured her. 'Lock up well and I'll use my key when I get back. I feel the need to stretch my legs.'

'That young lady who called yesterday,' Tilde said innocently, 'looks as if she'd wear high heels and ribbons in her hair just to fetch the groceries.'

'I can't say that I troubled to sum up her character,' Tansy said blandly. 'I'll be back in an hour or two.'

She took the side path a few yards from her house that brought her to the river bank and felt, as she always did, the return of optimism when she smelled the river breeze and saw the usual line of elderly fishermen seated in their accustomed places.

She and Frank had dropped into the habit, since they had become close friends, of often taking a walk along the river bank if his chanced to be an early evening visit. The last of the light playing on the water as it ebbed and flowed, the sudden dart of a fish above the surface or the twisting of an eel just below made it seem as if they were in genuine countryside, far removed from the crowded noisy city that was London.

'Though the charms of rural life would pretty soon pall for me,' Frank had admitted. 'I'm a born newspaper man and there's

127

always something happening in the metro-
polis.'

'There's probably just as much going on in
the country,' Tansy had argued.

'Only more slowly!' Frank had retorted and
the pair of them had burst out laughing.

Thinking of that now as she walked along
the darkening bank, Tansy found herself
smiling at that memory and memories of
other occasions when they had laughed and
joked together. She had told herself firmly
that they were as close as she might have been
to a brother had she ever had one, but the
comparison didn't please her so greatly now.

The recent rain had discouraged some of
the usual figures she saw seated with their
rods along the bank, perhaps because even
thick blankets and cushions placed on the
damp grass could not banish the lurking
threat of rheumatism that seemed to afflict
the old. At this point Tansy stopped to smile
at the way her thoughts were tending
— herself and Frank, both in their dotage,
seated behind their fishing rods on the banks
of the river and, no doubt, grumbling gently
about the ill manners of the younger
generation.

She was still smiling at her wayward
thoughts when a violent shove in her back
sent her into the river, her heavy skirts and

thick walking boots dragging her beneath the surface immediately.

For a moment she flailed wildly, gasping as water filled her mouth and eyes and nostrils, and then, the quick reactions on which she prided herself coming to her aid, she tugged at the belt that held her skirts snugly round her slim waist, kicked vigorously and rose to the surface, coughing and spluttering, her vision dimmed by the water, her long legs in their cotton drawers pedalling wildly as her boots threatened to drag her down again.

Her first instinct was to reach for the bank but an instant's thought caused her to hold her nose and her breath and allow herself to sink just beneath the surface again, where she floated with some difficulty to where a part of the bank encroached over the current and she was able to haul herself up with some difficulty.

Still coughing and spluttering, she pulled herself into a sitting position and looked back along the bank but it was deserted. Whoever had pushed her had departed as rapidly and silently as they had arrived without waiting to see the results of the onslaught.

The inside of her mouth and her throat seemed full of the dirty scum that floated along the surface. Tansy leaned over, stuck her finger down her throat, and vomited up a quantity of bilge. She could only hope that sufficient hadn't actually reached her stomach in any quantity that could infect her.

Apart from a few lamps glowing from the back windows of the houses and the occasional glint of light from a boat or skiff passing further along the river, twilight had become night with the moon hiding. This, she realized as she wiped her mouth on a handful of leaves she had pulled up, was proof surely that someone was aware of her investigations and wanted desperately for her to be stopped. That conclusion, which ought to have given her some satisfaction, only succeeded in making her feel extremely nervous.

Suddenly dreading the return of her assailant, who might want to satisfy himself that she was well and truly drowned, she turned and walked rapidly back towards her own house, grateful for the darkness that concealed the fact she was squelching along in waterlogged boots and her cotton drawers!

There was no hope of avoiding either Mrs Timothy or Tilde, who were both seated in the kitchen as she came round to the front of the house, the curtains still partly open since they liked to see who was passing from time to time and, she guessed, would be on the lookout for more mysterious intruders.

As she had expected, Tilde's startled face at

the window was succeeded by Tilde herself, who came rushing round to open the front door, a fount of questions on her lips.

'Oh, Miss Tansy! Whatever happened? Your skirts? You're all wet! What happened?'

'I fell in,' Tansy said grimly, stepping inside and allowing herself to drip on to the rug.

'In the river?' Tilde's eyes would have fallen out had she widened them more. 'Oh, Miss Tansy! How did you do that??'

'By overbalancing when I was standing on the edge of the bank,' Tansy told her. 'The ground is treacherous after the rain. Can you see about hot water and towels?'

'A wetting in the Thames,' pronounced Mrs Timothy, now making an appearance, 'is no laughing matter. That water is full of unclean things that oughtn't to be floating about. If you haven't caught your death of cold you've likely picked up the cholera or the typhus or at the least the rheumatism will set in your bones and — '

'And a hot toddy to follow my bath will be most welcome,' Tansy said, stopping to pull off her boots and starting up the stairs with as much dignity as her appearance would permit. Half an hour later, clad in a warm dressing gown, her feet encased in velvet slippers, she sat by the relighted fire in her sitting-room drinking the hot soup and toast that Mrs Timothy had insisted on augmenting with a glass of brandy.

'For though neither you nor I nor young Tilde indulge in the coarser pleasures, Miss Tansy, there's no denying that brandy, taken during emergencies and in strict moderation, can infuse body and spirits with a glow of good health and wellbeing,' she announced.

'The actual emergency,' Tansy said dryly, 'was when I fell into the river.'

'The aftershock can have some very nasty effects in the shape of breathlessness and trembling and the weakening of bones, especially in the back,' Mrs Timothy insisted.

Tansy, sipping soup and brandy, wondered idly if Mrs Timothy's bad back had been induced through falling in a river, but decided not to enquire.

Soon she had persuaded the pair of them to their respective rooms and was able to retrace her earlier actions in her mind. Someone had crept up and given her an almighty shove in the small of her back that had pitched her into the river. Not one of the venerable gentlemen who fished from the banks but whom the inclement rain had kept away, not a mischievous urchin or a thief since nothing had been snatched from her. There remained only the uncomfortable fact that someone wanted her permanently out of the way. Since she couldn't think of anybody who disliked her sufficiently to make an end of her, the reason for the attack could only be the investigation in which she was taking a modest part.

That meant that the deaths of Joseph Fanshaw and Brook Wilton had indeed been murder and that someone was well aware that she was involved in the case. She debated with herself whether or not to tell her father or Frank of the recent incident and decided against it.

Laurence would insist on Finn accompanying her everywhere and Frank would hang around, no doubt dreaming of brunettes in pink dresses, while his own good nature would force him to look after the safety of a good friend.

Having reached that stage in her reasoning she yawned, finished off the brandy and betook herself to bed where, rather to her surprise, she slept dreamlessly until morning.

'I think it best,' she cautioned her staff of two before she left for the museum, 'if neither of you ever mentions the fact that I was silly enough to tumble into the river. Pa would only fret himself with the fact that even had he been there he would've been unable to help and Mr Frank would tease the life out of me for being so clumsy.'

Both nodded solemnly, though as she left the house she heard Mrs Timothy say, a sniff in her voice, 'Solitary walks indeed! What Miss Tansy needs is a nice solid husband to walk between her and any river she happens to be wandering along!'

And Tilde's voice replied, 'I begin to think Miss Tansy's heart is in the grave with her late intended. It's lucky she is not living in Paris for there are so many bridges across the Seine that it positively encourages people to jump in. Poor dear Mama often said — '

What poor dear Mama had often said was destined to remain unheard as Tansy closed the front door and walked briskly down the path.

Mr Benson was already behind his glass partition when she reached the museum. He favoured her with a nod and a faint smile as she handed over the keys and looked, she thought, almost approving as he handed her in return a sheaf of brochures.

'If you will check the information in these with the artefacts that are actually in the display cases,' he said, 'our visitors will have a much clearer idea of our resources. One does become weary of visitors claiming the information is out of date.'

Meaning, she guessed, that one lone complaint had been received during the previous twelve months! Glancing from the curling up ends of the brochures to his spare, thin frame she again had the impression that he was drying up along with the museum.

At least he hadn't made any awkward enquiries as to whether or not she had been up into the storeroom before the weekend and she went off comfortably enough to make a spot check of the exhibits with the feeling that before another week had elapsed she would probably know them by heart.

Mr Benson received them, neatly corrected, back from her just before he went across the road for his luncheon, nodding approval.

'I believe I can safely say that I am not dissatisfied with your performance so far,' he said somewhat grudgingly. 'Now I will leave you to get on with the usual dusting and do please ensure the Do Not Touch notices are prominently displayed. The general public is apt to be very thoughtless in that respect!'

Since the general public consisted that day of two elderly ladies who exchanged recipes for marmalade as they walked through the rooms, Tansy thought the warning a trifle unnecessary, but she nodded gravely and watched him with almost maternal solicitude as he put on his hat and sallied forth to the café.

Leaving the two visitors to argue amiably over the respective merits of ginger marmalade and the more customary orange flavour she betook herself to the small room near the staircase at the back and, taking out a small notebook, began to scribble a few observations, reminding herself as she did so that these were merely to stimulate her own thinking. Had she allowed Laurence a glimpse of them he would've told her bluntly they looked amateurish.

★ ★ ★

Joseph Fanshaw and Brook Wilton, two assistant curators in different museums and not as far as I know acquaintances or friends. Died within a couple of weeks of each other of apparent gastric fever, this verdict now being questioned after Miss Susan Harris received a letter on her return to the Kensington Museum, having nursed her aunt, from Brook Wilton hinting at his suspicion his illness was not naturally induced.

Both young men according to their landladies were quiet and respectable, no family or friends and, it seems, no vices! Now authorities are considering an exhumation.

Carl Royston, millionaire, Viennese background, wife named Vashti from Middle East. One son, nothing known of him. Wife left him after five years for another man. Word Vashti underlined in red in Bible belonging to Joseph Fanshaw — landlady. Heavily varnished wooden case (?) found in storeroom in rough shape of female figure. Finn seeing to that.

Tilde complained of being followed home. Note — Tilde has vivid imagination but is not a liar. Self had exactly same sentiments the other evening but unable to verify impression. However no doubt that someone whom Tilde mistook for me entered my bedroom through open window, witness broken creepers, lit the lamp, took one kid glove from my drawer and went out through verandah doors.

Also no doubt that while standing on the river-bank I received a violent push in the back which sent me into the river. Managed to unhook my skirt and struggle to surface by which time assailant had gone. Cannot think it was casual attack and certainly not attempted robbery.

★   ★   ★

Neither, she thought, chewing the end of her pencil thoughtfully, could she imagine what she could have possibly found out that might induce anybody to try to murder her.

The sound of Mr Benson's returning footsteps galvanized her into getting up and tucking both notebook and pencil hastily away as the two recipe-exchanging ladies trotted through to the reception area again.

'You may go for your lunch now,' Mr Benson said, nodding approvingly as she smiled the two ladies out. 'I rather fear we shall have no more visitors today. Monday is often a quiet day for many people like to do their shopping and of course in many households it's washday too. One cannot expect people to flock to the museum.'

He sounded regretful, as if the place really meant something to him. Tansy murmured some reply and hastened to put on her hat.

The little café was as dull as the museum with its unvarying menu of eggs, boiled, poached or scrambled, its pork pies and its cabbage and potato soup. Tansy bought a couple of buttered scones and a pot of tea and sat down to partake of what Finn would have regarded as a shamefully frugal repast when a shadow fell across her.

'Miss Clark?'

Tansy looked up into the expressionless face of a man in livery. For an instant she stared at him blankly and then she recognized the footman who had admitted her to Royston House.

'You come from Mr Royston,' she said instantly.

'Yes, Miss Clark.' For an instant he permitted a flicker of gratification to cross his face before he said in his stiff manner, 'Mr Royston requests the pleasure of your company for coffee at his residence.'

'I'm supposed to be working,' she began.

'I have already informed Mr Benson that you will not be returning to work until tomorrow,' he informed her.

Typical high-handedness on Carl Royston's part, she thought with a flush of indignation. However, he wasn't apparently about to dismiss her! She pushed her half-finished snack aside and reached for her purse.

'The bill is already paid, Miss Clark,' the footman said.

'Thank you, Mr . . . ?'

'James, Miss Clark, without the prefix.' For a moment a gleam of humour showed in the cold eyes, 'All footmen, you are aware, are called James.'

'Yes, of course.'

Suppressing her own chuckle, she rose and allowed herself to be ushered along the street and into a private carriage, as sleek and undecorated as the exterior of the mansion where Carl Royston lived in solitary splendour.

A coachman was already waiting to urge on the horses and James, having politely assisted her within, shut the door and climbed up beside the driver.

Coach and horses, Tansy thought, determined not to be impressed. In this age of steam and electrical power with horseless vehicles predicted!

Nevertheless it was pleasant to be treated like a young woman of consequence. She even felt a mild regret that she hadn't worn her new pink outfit.

When they reached Royston House, James assisted her down into the courtyard and escorted her to a side door from which they traversed a short passage which brought them into the main hall.

'Mr Royston is in the small salon, Miss Clark,' James informed her. 'This ·way, please.'

Carl Royston was seated in a high-backed chair cushioned in velvet of the same soft grey as the curtains at the long windows and the rugs scattered over the floor. A fire crackled merrily in the hearth but the room itself retained an air of cool tranquillity. The panelled walls were bare of ornament save for a round mirror bordered with carved leaves and twigs in some kind of shiny white wood.

'Not wood, Miss Clark,' her host said, using his silver-topped stick to rise, and giving the answer to her unspoken assumption. 'Bones. Human bones. French bones.'

'Bones!' Echoing the word, Tansy stared at the mirror and found it much less attractive than she had first thought.

'During the wars with France at the beginning of this century,' Carl Royston said, looking faintly amused at her expression, 'many French soldiers and sailors were held prisoner along the South Wales coast. Many died in prison. Those left behind collected the bones of their comrades and decorated mirrors with them, small jewel boxes and the like. It's said such objects bring ill luck but I have always scorned superstition. Coffee?'

'Thank you,' Tansy said, averting her eyes from the weirdly decorated mirror.

'William Benson has given me a favourable report of your work,' he was continuing, resuming his chair and beckoning her to a similar seat opposite him, both chairs being within easy reaching distance of a round table on which the modest repast was laid. 'We will dispense with formality and help ourselves. I say 'work' but I am well aware of the fact that the help of an assistant curator is scarcely necessary. But then that isn't why you are at the museum in the first place, is it? You are looking into something on your admirable father's behalf. I shall be most interested to hear what it is.'

He set down his untasted coffee and stared at her out of bright, gleaming eyes.

9

'People,' Tansy said somewhat breathlessly, 'can get exceedingly bored without working.'

'I doubt if a bored person would choose to work in a museum visited by few people,' Carl Royston said dryly. 'You are a woman of moderate but independent means. You would have chosen another theatre for your talents, so I repeat, what exactly are you doing in my museum?'

'You never visit it yourself, Mr Royston,' she evaded.

'Once I have set events in motion,' he told her, 'I leave the day-to-day running of places to others.'

'But to visit occasionally — '

'Miss Clark, I have founded three small museums,' he said impatiently. 'A centre for indigent women and an art gallery, not to mention the fact I hold directorships in museums in Vienna, Heidelberg, Paris and Kensington — '

'Kensington?' Tansy interjected sharply.

'Where the assistant curator died apparently of gastric fever, very soon after the assistant curator in my Chelsea museum expired of the same apparent cause. Two young healthy men, working in different museums die of the same illness at a time when there is no outbreak of that illness. I do not believe in impossible coincidences, Miss Clark, but both had been visited by eminently respectable and fully qualified doctors in the days before their deaths. Certainly there were no grounds to demand an autopsy. Yet the coincidence nagged at me. Then you arrived at my house, seeking a post at the Chelsea museum. You had no formal training: the post of assistant curator had not yet been advertised, yet there you were! I decided to employ you though I was sure you had some other plan in mind. Fortunately also, since for years I have kept myself informed as to the progress of your father, it occurred to me that you might be bound on the same quest I myself was contemplating.'

'What did you plan to do?' Tansy asked.

'I had no plans! I had formulated nothing and then you arrived to ask for a job like the answer to a prayer, though praying is not a habit of mine. I recognized the name of Clark and you bear a certain likeness to your father. I decided that what you found out would reach my ears sooner or later. So, Miss Clark, what have you discovered so far?'

He had leaned forward suddenly, gripping

144

his silver-handled stick, his eyes fixed unwaveringly on her face. For an instant she felt a tremor of something akin to fear. Then her usual good sense reasserted itself. If Carl Royston was in the habit of intimidating people in order to obtain what he wanted, she was not going to oblige him.

'Let me tell you something,' he said as she remained silent. 'When I was a young man I travelled extensively. My father was wealthy and indulged me greatly. My English mother adored me. I was her only child and her pride in me was immense. After every trip to foreign parts I would make it my pleasure to return to her and tell her what I had seen. Always I brought back presents that I knew she would like. When she died it was a blow almost past enduring, worse even than the death of my father. He was an excellent man but our relationship was more formal, more Austrian if you like.'

For the first time, Tansy thought, he sounded almost human. Whatever gentleness lay buried in his nature owed its existence to his mother, she guessed.

As if he sensed her reaction he straightened up sharply in his chair, and after a brief pause continued.

'However, I had excellent health and my enterprises were flourishing. There were still many places I had never visited, much that I had read about but never seen. I went to Egypt, to Palestine, to Syria. I met my wife in Persia. I was forty-eight years old and a settled bachelor. She was eighteen and quite exquisite. I wanted above all other ambitions to possess her.'

Tansy winced inwardly, disliking the word 'possess'.

'Darkly beautiful with classic features and a family who were unwilling to allow her to wed any of the local suitors but looked higher for her. And she seemed to admire me, Miss Clark. I paid double the bride price and brought her back to England. I dressed her like a queen, bought her the finest jewels, introduced her into the best society, After five years she deserted me.'

'I'm very sorry,' Tansy said uncomfortably.

She wanted to ask about the son but he had made an impatient motion with his hand as if he disliked talking further about personal matters.

'These things happen,' he said. 'A great difference in age, younger admirers. I made extensive enquiries as to her whereabouts but with no positive result. After her departure I heard of a statue of the original Queen Vashti. It had been found in some tomb, by grave-robbers no doubt; had passed through several hands and then had disappeared again. I made up my mind that as I had lost the living Vashti it was my right to possess the statue. A whim if you like to call it so, Miss Clark.'

'Whim', she thought uneasily, didn't sound like quite the right word. There was anger here mingled with greed and an uncontrollable desire to get one's way.

'The cabinet,' she said instead. 'That beautifully carved cabinet in the large room — '

'I had it designed and made for the figure,' he said.

'But if it was only a rumour — '

'Rumour counts for much in the ancient world. I was sure the statue existed and so I made a home for it. Great discoveries are made through rumour, Miss Clark. Legendary cities are excavated because a camel driver gossips with his neighbour or a man gets tipsy in a tavern and lets fall some gossip he had heard. Not all treasures are displayed for the public to gape at. And this was a rare find — too rare to be announced.'

'So you had the cabinet made before you knew whether or not it really existed or whether it would ever belong to you?'

'I sensed that it existed and I decided that one day it would belong to me,' he said.

There was a cold implacability in his face and voice that made her heart quail.

'Was it said to be very old?' she ventured.

'From what I heard through various sources at various times it had been excavated in Persia. It may originally have formed part of the lost treasures of Jerusalem. Various stories were blown like sand across the desert. I heard also that it had been found in some rich woman's tomb. Think of it lying there for centuries before I met the living Vashti and married her!'

Tansy stared at him, fascinated despite herself by the tone of his voice and the glitter of his eyes. He looked and sounded like a man caught in the toils of some unbearable desire.

'There was even talk of the Persian government claiming it,' he continued. 'Then ensued a long silence, only the occasional vague rumour that it had passed through many hands. There were times when I feared that I would never see it, never own it.'

'And then?'

She shrank inwardly from the naked greed in his eyes but something made her respond.

'About twelve years ago,' he said, 'I learned that it had been smuggled out of the Middle East and been passed from country to country. Many who claimed to know where it was died under mysterious circumstances or disappeared themselves. However, I had what I believed to be reliable information that it had been taken to the Caribbean and was in Jamaica.'

'Jamaica?' The word made her jump slightly.

'A man called — well, his name is not important — died out there shortly after gaining possession of the statue and the statue itself disappeared again. Since then I have waited for it to surface again, perhaps in some obscure sale, perhaps as part of a thieves' hoard. That it still exists I know as surely as I know my own name and nature.'

'Did you know — ' she began and stopped, aware that his eyes held a certain grim amusement.

'That your fiancé had died of the yellow fever out in Jamaica, yes. That he had left you comfortably settled, yes. Of course I learned this some years later and then I began to make logical deductions.'

'You thought that Geoffrey had the figure and had willed it to me? I can assure you that he did not,' she said flatly.

'It was also possible that he owned it without knowing what it was. Such things have happened in the past. Dear old ladies put some priceless object on a bring-and-buy stall in support of the local church, not knowing they are parting with a king's ransom! It took a long time to make the necessary arrangements for unfortunately my health is not what it was and my age too counts against me when it comes to travelling without a veritable retinue of servants. But you know, Miss Clark, in this wicked world anyone, provided they have the means, can buy anything and anyone. Avarice and corruption are bedfellows in every land.'

'And some people never can be bought,' Tansy said.

'How idealistic you are, my dear Miss Clark,' he said, amused. 'I promise you that money talks louder than anything else in the world and smells sweeter than love.'

'Mr Royston, I really don't want to hear any more!' Tansy said abruptly, starting to rise. At that moment she could sense corruption and avarice and wanted to breathe clean air.

'But you have only heard half the tale,' he said. 'Joseph Fanshaw and Brook Wilton were in the Chelsea and Kensington museums because I arranged for them to be appointed. They were there to look out for any clue as to the statue's whereabouts. I have other — shall we call them helpers — in other museums, others travelling the world, ostensibly tourists on a limited income but with their eyes open and their ears strained to catch the merest hint of a whisper. It has already cost me a fortune.'

'Which might've been better employed in other causes!' Tansy said sharply.

'If the poor have not the brains and the valour to raise themselves then it is useless to throw more money after them,' he said impatiently. 'But we're straying from the subject! The two men who died — '

'I understand that the authorities are considering exhumation and an autopsy,' she told him reluctantly. 'I would have thought you already knew that.'

'I am a director of the Kensington Museum but I don't involve myself often with the day-to-day running of the place except on rare occasions. So the authorities also have grown suspicious of two deaths when no epidemic existed? I thought it likely. If both of them had stumbled across information and unwisely delayed making it known to me — '

'You think they were killed because they had information about the statue? Is that what you're saying?'

'You're an intelligent woman but not as sharp as your father.' He leaned back in his chair and surveyed her with amusement. 'I noticed that keen-faced, red-haired officer when some coins were stolen from my collection here. Over the years since I've occasionally considered whether or not to consult him on the matter of the statue, but did nothing about it. Your father is not in a position when he can travel easily abroad. I employed others for that purpose.'

'To go to Jamaica?'

'Indeed yes! Of course twelve years ago, when the whisper the statue was in Jamaica first came to my ears, I immediately sent scouts to survey the territory, so to speak.'

'I'm surprised you didn't go yourself,' Tansy said.

'Oh, physically I was perfectly capable of making the journey,' he nodded, 'but why would Carl Royston suddenly arrive in Kingston on the heels of a rumour? No, I employed deputies. One doesn't keep dogs and bark oneself.'

'And the people you employed found . . . '

'That your fiancé, name of — well, the name doesn't matter — '

'It mattered to me!' Tansy broke in, her hands automatically clenching into fists. 'It still matters to me but that's because I regard people as human beings, not as objects to be used and thrown aside. Geoffrey was my fiancé, Mr Royston, and he went back to Jamaica to settle his late father's estate! He had no interest in stolen artefacts. He loved going round museums, and he had taught himself a lot from books. And, yes, he had visited the Middle East on a few occasions before we met and became engaged, but it's utterly ridiculous to suggest he might've been involved with grave-robbers and crooks!'

'But if the statue had come into his hands by chance might he not have hidden it and gone out to Jamaica to retrieve it?'

'It's simply nonsense! Geoffrey travelled quite often and published several travel articles in various periodicals but he went to settle — '

'His father's estate and died of yellow fever.'

'Yes,' she said flatly, suddenly feeling a hopelessness settle over her.

'The statue wasn't in his grave, Miss Clark,' Carl Royston said.

'What?' Raising her head, she stared at him.

'All recent deaths in the area where the statue was rumoured to be were naturally investigated by my employees,' he told her. 'The statue was not in your fiancé's grave.'

'I don't believe this,' she said painfully. 'I don't believe people would open — '

'My dear Miss Clark, how do you suppose half the treasures of Egypt were found?' he said. The amusement had crept into his face again.

'Forgive me but I have to go!'

Sick and shaken, she rose jerkily to her feet.

'And it's clear from your transparent honesty — most refreshing in this corrupt age! — that the whereabouts of the statue and the rumour that your late fiancé was involved with it came as a complete surprise to you,' he said benignly.

'Mr Royston,' Tansy said tensely, 'I have decided to terminate my employment at the Chelsea Museum. I will work out the remainder of this week and after that I shall regard the whole matter closed and any further communication between us out of the question. Perhaps you ought to visit the place yourself one day. Hardly anyone else does since the displays are so very unimaginative, but I daresay you are too busy arranging for graves to be robbed!'

Without waiting for a reply she crossed the room, opened the door, resisted the childish impulse to slam it, walked across the hall and was about to struggle with the heavy front door when James emerged from quarters obscure, drew the bolts, and bade her good day in his most expressionless manner.

Geoffrey's grave had been opened shortly after his death and obviously violated. On the instructions of a wealthy, evil old man who wanted to lock the replica of his wife up in a case and hide her for ever from the world as he had never been able to do in reality.

At least she wasn't expected back at the museum that day! The thought of continuing with dreary routine when her whole being blazed with anger and disgust was more than she could bear.

She walked briskly towards the nearest cab-stand, feeling the cool air fan her flushed cheeks, her bag swinging from her arm.

As she turned the corner, a familiar voice hailed her from across the road and Frank darted out, deftly avoiding the oncoming traffic.

'Don't tell me!' he greeted her cheerfully. 'You're in this part of town because Carl Royston has put you in sole charge of his museum!'

To save her life she couldn't have embarked on a genuine explanation at that moment. Instead she said as lightly as her mood would allow, 'I went to see Carl Royston to give in my notice. I'll work out the rest of the week but I'm positive there's nothing more to find out that would have any bearing on our inquiry.'

'If you're sure?' He shot her a doubtful look.

'Come to that,' she said, still lightly, 'What are you doing here?'

'I've been speaking to the chief coroner.' He drew her arm though his.

'And?'

'The powers-that-be have ordered an exhumation of both bodies.'

'Because of the letter Brook Wilton sent to Susan Harris?' Effectively diverted, she stopped dead and stared at him.

'That set the ball rolling,' he told her, 'but when both doctors, each of whom had attended one of the assistant curators, were interviewed, both agreed separately that there were some unusual features in each of the cases which, had they been aware of the other case, would have led them to hesitate before issuing a death certificate. The exhumation takes place privately this evening. Since the two were buried in separate cemeteries I will be running between the two in my capacity as newspaper reporter. I don't suppose you would care to — ?'

'No, thank you!' Tansy said decidedly.

'Anyway, I am on my way to your pa's house to give him the news. I'm hoping he will agree to postpone our visit there to find out what Finn has made of that wooden casing until tomorrow. I know it's irritating of me and you will be able to tell me everything but I do rather enjoy being a personal spectator.'

'And tomorrow you might be able to tell us the results of the autopsies. I suppose they will be carried out quickly?'

'Immediately, as far as I know. Are you coming to see Laurence?'

'No,' Tansy said. 'Tell him that I'll see him tomorrow evening. Right now, I feel rather tired to tell you the truth. Ah! here comes a vacant cab! Bye, Frank!'

She waved the cab down and climbed inside, wanting at that moment only to be alone in a quiet place where she could banish from her mind the picture of another grave being dug up beneath the hot Jamaican sun.

10

'I will be sorry to lose you, Miss Clark,' William Benson said the next morning when she arrived at the museum. 'Mr Royston has sent word that you find the work somewhat tedious and have decided to leave on Friday. I told him frankly that I found no fault beyond a certain regrettable tendency to allow your sense of humour mastery over your finer instincts and that the habit could be eradicated in time, but it seems you are resolved?'

'Actually,' Tansy said confidingly, 'I have found the museum quite an interesting place but it has forced me to cut down on my charity work.'

Obviously Mr Royston hadn't taken the curator into his full confidence. On impulse she enquired, 'I suppose your own work here is more varied — I mean, when new artefacts are delivered? To decide where they are to go and to catalogue them?'

'Very few artefacts are delivered here, Miss Clark.' He sounded regretful. 'Usually on the rare occasions that occurs Mr Royston himself is present at the delivery but of recent years he has lost his initial enthusiasm for the place. He has other interests, of course, and his age is telling upon him, but it is a pity.'

'Yes indeed,' she said absently.

Had Carl Royston genuinely lost interest in his museum or was that merely a blind to conceal his true intentions? Whatever they might be!

'But we must get on!' he said briskly as if long lines of visitors thronged the street. 'I think the glass cases might benefit from a little extra polishing today and with the schools all open again we might expect several parties of children very soon.'

He might expect them but she doubted if any would come. Nevertheless she collected her dusters and beeswax and went obediently to work, pausing only to give Antonio a friendly nod.

Going across to the café to eat her own luncheon snack, she half expected to see James waiting to whisk her off to Royston House again, but she finished her pork pie and was drinking her coffee when the welcome figure of Frank Cartwright hovered in the doorway, raised his hand in greeting and came over to her.

'I'll join you for a beer,' he said. 'Watching grave-digging leaves a nasty taste in the mouth. I thought you might like to hear the results.'

'Of the autopsies? They've done them already?'

'Two of the top London pathologists worked through the rest of the night, each one on a separate corpse after which they compared findings. Incidentally, dashing back and forth between cemeteries isn't my favourite way of spending an evening!'

'Never mind that!' Tansy said abruptly, closing her mind to the all-too-vivid picture his words conjured up. 'What were the results of the autopsies?'

'Both Joseph Fanshaw and Brook Wilton died of antimony poisoning,' Frank said.

'Antimony! Antimony can bring about apparent symptoms of gastric fever,' Tansy said. 'I recall my mother and Pa discussing a similar case some years ago.'

How well she could remember herself curled up in a chair, a piece of tedious needlework in her hands, while her parents discussed the merits and demerits of various cases in which her father was professionally involved! Her mother had been a dainty woman, her lace collars always pristine, her crinoline billowing around her, as she listened eagerly to her husband expound his theories.

'Tansy?'

Frank was looking at her. She pulled her mind back into the present.

'So two assistant curators have been poisoned by antimony,' she said thoughtfully. 'As far as we know they weren't personally acquainted though their characters and circumstances were very similar. Young men without families or sweethearts, living in separate parts of the city, quiet, respectable lodgers. If Brook Wilton had felt his illness might not be gastric fever and had written a note to Susan Harris, why didn't he mention it to the doctor?'

'Doctors don't usually encourage their patients to diagnose themselves,' Frank said drily. 'It was just a pity that the note to Susan Harris arrived too late.'

'Have you told her yet about the results?'

'This evening when she finishes work,' he said, 'I'm taking her for a light meal and I'll tell her then. I may be a trifle late arriving at Laurence's.'

'You saw him last night?'

'Very briefly, merely to tell Finn to let him know we'd be there tonight to find out if he'd made any sense of the wooden casing.'

'Yes, of course.' The thought of the exhumations and autopsies had driven the wooden figure out of her mind. Now with something of an effort she said, 'I take it that

Finn hasn't managed to open it yet — if it does open.'

'He's getting the varnish off it and enjoying being mysterious,' Frank said with a grin. 'I assume it's not been missed yet?'

'I doubt if it ever would be,' Tansy said consideringly. 'The storeroom is just a jumble of rubbish. Mr Benson has nothing to do with any artefacts which are delivered and hardly any have been delivered for years as far as I can learn.'

'Yet someone made a secret hiding place in the wall and put the figure there. Well, we may know more tonight.'

'I take it that you won't be eating at Pa's?' she queried, hoping he didn't notice the slight asperity in her tone. 'If you are taking Miss Harris — ?'

'For a late tea or a very early supper, whichever you please to call it,' Frank said cheerfully with no sign of embarrassment. 'I won't be able to write up recent events until the matter is made public. At the moment the investigation proceeds in strict secrecy. Apart from the designated authorities only you, your pa, Finn and I know about it.'

'And Susan Harris.'

'And Susan Harris,' he amended. 'Since she brought the letter scrawled by Brook Wilton to notice she is hardly likely to have gone round poisoning people with antimony. Will I see you around nine? I can call — '

'I think you'd best see Miss Harris safely to her lodgings first,' Tansy said. 'I will get a cab and see you at Pa's.'

She went on smiling cheerfully as he rose, turned to lift his hand at the door and went out into the street again.

Whatever his professional reasons, Frank was obviously charmed by Susan Harris, and why — she asked herself bleakly — shouldn't he be? She was darkly pretty, smaller than Tansy and about ten years younger, and more feminine, obviously, or Frank wouldn't have been at such pains to look after her properly.

Returning to the museum she tried to interest herself in the rearrangement of some Bronze Age necklaces, held a silent debate with Antonio as to whether he'd enjoyed being a soldier in the Roman Army, and thankfully resumed her outdoor clothes when Mr Benson informed her that it was closing time.

It wasn't until she reached her own house that she realized she had been so busy listening to Frank's news, she had completely neglected to tell him more about her interview with Carl Royston. The theories he had laid before her, his notion that Geoffrey might've been involved in the robbing of graves, the fact that Geoffrey's own resting place had been violated, were things she hoped to keep from her father and Frank as long as possible.

By the time she had changed her dress for one her father liked because it was the same dark blue as her mother had often worn, drunk some tea and succumbed to Tilde's plea to 'have a nice buttered scone with it, Miss Tansy! With autumn upon us and winter round the corner we have to keep up our strength, so Mrs Timothy says!' it was past 7.30.

Though the last light was fading fast, the rain had held off and when she walked round to the river-bank she was pleased to see several of the usual fishermen in their places. At least there was small chance of anyone shoving her into the water again, she thought, deliberately keeping a wide margin between herself and the reed-fringed edges of the bank where it sloped steeply into the river. She had a further safeguard. Tucked into her pocket, her hand resting lightly on the butt, reposed her pistol, making hardly a bulge but primed and loaded.

There was plenty of time before she needed to get a cab to her father's place. She would decide when she got there exactly how much to tell him about her interview with Carl

Royston. Pa had really taken to Geoffrey, had treated him like a son, and the thought of his violated grave would affect him greatly. Since it had transpired that nothing of value had been found there then she might never tell him at all.

The moon had risen, silvering the water, haloing the bushes and the trees that afforded some privacy to the backs of the houses flanking the river-bank. Slightly ahead of her a stream bubbled into the river proper, the path interrupted by a wooden footbridge with a sturdy rail.

Even as she set her foot upon the wooden planks she heard the soft scrape of a shoe just behind her. Without pausing she turned, holding the pistol steady as she drew it from her pocket, cocked it, staring at the figure that stood before her, apparently transformed into stone at the sight of the weapon.

'Don't shoot, Miss Clark!' a voice shuddered out as two arms were hastily raised heavenwards.

'Who on earth are you?' Tansy demanded, her own heart thudding.

The moon, blazing whitely forth, eradicated shadows and rendered faces white blanks without any distinguishing features.

'Robert Blake, if you please, Miss Clark,' a voice, masculine and young, answered her.

'Who the devil is — You're the butcher's boy!'

'His son, actually, Miss Clark.' There was a touch of hurt pride in the youth's voice. 'One day, when I'm 21, which is in a few months' time, Dad's going to have Blake and Son put over the front of the shop.'

'Then why on earth are you following me?' Tansy demanded. 'Did Tilde put you up to it?'

'No, Miss Tansy! It was only that sometimes I like to take a walk along the river-bank when work's over for the day,' he said, arms still in the air.

'Put your arms down, for heaven's sake!' Tansy said irritably, replacing the weapon in her pocket. 'What do you want? Why are you on the river-bank anyway?'

'Sometimes when I walk here,' Robert Blake said shyly, 'I catch a glimpse of Tilde. Your back garden runs down almost to the river and often she comes out for a breath of air. Once or twice we've exchanged a few words over the garden wall — all very respectful, like.'

'Have you indeed?' Tansy said, stifling amusement. 'So why follow me this evening — or are you in the habit of following sundry ladies and girls up and down river-banks?'

'Oh no, Miss Clark!' He sounded shocked.

'Truth is that I've never had a proper sweetheart. Too busy with the carving of joints and the learning of the retail side of things to spare much time for anything else, but Tilde, she's different, isn't she? Not just very pretty and very sweet, but well born too. Did you know her father was a French aristocrat?'

'I have heard something of the kind,' Tansy said.

'Not that she's proud of it in a high-handed way or anything!' he rushed on. 'She isn't a snob! After all, when her family lost their fortune she had to come here and earn her living just like the rest of us. And she barely remembers Paris.'

Since Tansy knew that Tilde had never set foot in France in her life, though she believed fervently that her late mother had, this came as no surprise. Tansy choked back a sudden spurt of laughter and said severely, 'So why are you following me?'

'To ask you — since in a manner of speaking you're her guardian — to ask you if I might start — well, you know.'

'Until you tell me no, I don't know,' Tansy said.

'If I could take her for a bit of a walk and perhaps a glass of lemonade and some cake sometime when she's not tied up with her household duties?'

'What you mean,' Tansy said helpfully, 'is whether or not I allow followers. Mr Blake, this is 1875. We are moving into the last quarter of the nineteenth century and my own opinion is that we should move with the times. If Tilde is willing to become more closely acquainted with you then I see no reason why she should not. She will be 21 very soon and then, provided she carries out her work satisfactorily, as she always has, her private time is her own. However, I hope you will remember that she is a young lady and treat her with respect?'

From the little Tilde recalled of her own mother, that lady — although susceptible to men claiming French blood — had been rather far from being a lady in any sense.

'Oh, indeed I will, Miss Clark!' he assured her fervently.

'In that case,' Tansy said, trying desperately to sound middle-aged and wise, 'Tilde usually has a couple of hours off in the evenings but seldom goes anywhere. If you wish to take her for a coffee and cake somewhere or for a walk then you may tell her you have my permission to ask her but the answer lies with her.'

'Thank you, Miss Clark!'

The moon had gentled a little and she could discern what she had noticed idly before on the rare occasions she had noticed him in his father's shop. He was a good-looking young man, not tall but well-built with character in his face.

'One other thing!' She delayed him as he turned to walk back along the bank. 'When you do invite Tilde it might be diplomatic to bring my housekeeper, Mrs Timothy, a couple of nice lamb chops or some of those herb sausages your father makes so excellently, and don't forget to ask how her back is. I'm very much afraid she will tell you but you will reckon it a small price to pay for standing high in her favour.'

'Miss Clark, shall I walk back with you now?' he asked abruptly.

'If you wish. I'm going out directly to visit my father but — '

'It wasn't just about Tilde and me that I came after you,' he said. 'There was a man following you, Miss Clark.'

'Along the bank? Surely not!'

'He kept close to the garden walls and the trees and shrubbery at the backs of the houses,' Robert Blake said. 'I noticed him particular because he moved very fast between the trees, like he was hiding from someone.'

'Did you see him clearly?'

The young man shook his head. 'Not as far

as I know,' he said, 'but the moonlight makes everything look queer and a bit spooky. But he was keeping just a few yards behind you only further over to your left. Then I got here on the bridge and you pointed a pistol at me. Is it real?'

'Indeed it is,' Tansy said firmly.

'And you carry it with you when you come out for a walk? I had heard that crime was getting worse but Chelsea has always been such a peaceful place! Ought not Tilde to carry — ?'

'No indeed!' Tansy said hastily. 'There's no need whatsoever for Tilde to go about armed! In any case she never does go out after dusk and when in future she does I trust you will be there to protect her without the use of firearms!'

'With my fists, Miss Clark! With my fists!' Robert Blake said fiercely.

'Excellent!' Tansy said heartily. 'Now perhaps you will be kind enough to walk with me to the cab-stand. I have an evening engagement.'

The idea of the over-imaginative and impulsive Tilde trotting round Chelsea either with a gun or accompanied by an armed suitor wasn't one she wanted to contemplate too closely.

As to who the mysterious follower had

been it was possible that Robert Blake had been mistaken but it was equally possible that she herself was being relentlessly trailed. She wondered with a shudder what his motive could be.

'I shall call upon Tilde tomorrow morning,' Robert said as he handed Tansy into a cab,

'With chops for Mrs Timothy?' she reminded him.

'Chops and sausages!' he assured her with a quick glancing smile.

Tansy felt a tiny pang, quickly suppressed, at the thought of Tilde being courted by a pleasant lad who clearly adored her. There had once been a time . . . she compressed her lips and stared fixedly through the cab window at the teeming streets.

When she reached her father's house, Finn was on hand to open the door and give her to understand by dint of nods and winks that he had information to impart.

'I too have something to tell,' Tansy informed him.

It was time to tell them, she had decided, about the mysterious figure with the glove glimpsed on the dark stairs by Tilde and about the two occasions on the river-bank when she had been almost drowned and followed with what she feared was no good intent.

'You're late!' Laurence greeted her when she entered the long sitting room.

'I was delayed,' she told him. 'Hello, Frank!'

'I've been telling your father the results of the autopsies,' Frank said. 'The whole business is being kept out of the public eye for the moment.'

'But you have been invited to consider the matter?' She gave her father an affectionate look.

'I have been asked to apply my mind to recent events,' he agreed modestly.

'I have other recent events to relate,' she told him.

'You can tell me while we eat,' he rejoined. 'Finn has news of his own for after the meal and is fairly bursting with the need to tell it.'

'I can bide in patience until Miss Tansy has spoken,' Finn said, entering with a laden tray of salads and cold meats. 'You'll excuse me if this is a bit of a scratch supper so to say but I've been pretty hard occupied these last days.'

'The meal looks very appetizing,' Laurence assured him. 'Now, Tansy, what information do you have to gladden our hearts.'

'I'm not sure if your hearts are going to be particularly gladdened by what I have to tell,' she responded doubtfully.

'Sounds ominous!' Frank said, passing her the bread rolls.

'Oh, the first episode was — well, anyway!' She launched into a recital of when Tilde had mistaken the intruder for herself.

'Whoever it was came in through the bedroom window, took one of my gloves and was on his way downstairs when Tilde came into the hall and then he — '

'Or she?' put in Laurence.

'Or she abruptly turned as if they were going up the stairs, came down again the moment that Tilde went into the kitchen and then let themselves out through the French windows, either dropping or leaving the glove they'd taken on the way out.'

'I would say left the glove,' Laurence said. 'The whole episode seems to me to have been staged to frighten you — possibly from continuing any more enquiries?'

'And the second episode?' Frank was looking at her keenly.

'Rather more alarming though I must admit I panicked.'

She told the story of the attack on the river-bank, softening the details of her struggles in the water, but conscious of the deep concern in the faces of all three who listened to her.

'You should have told me immediately,'

Laurence said sternly. 'I have only one daughter of whom I happen to be rather fond. You had no right to keep this to yourself, Tansy.'

'I take it that you won't be taking any more evening strolls along the river?' Frank said.

Tansy, who had been going to tell them what Robert Blake had seen, held her peace.

'This is serious,' Laurence frowned. 'Quite clearly someone is fully aware that Tansy is looking into recent happenings connected with the museum.'

'And for the moment the authorities have decided to keep the results of the autopsies under wraps,' Frank supplied. 'I can see that might lull the murderer into a sense of false security but if he already knows that Tansy is involved in a private investigation then the situation is dangerous.'

'Which is why I've taken to carrying my pistol about with me,' Tansy said.

'Small consolation,' Frank muttered.

'There's fruit and cheese for pudding,' Finn said. 'No time to make anything more. It's been a busy weekend for me.'

'And you are longing to show us the results,' Tansy said. 'I'm sorry, Finn. I didn't mean to steal your thunder!'

'Miss Tansy, you can steal anything from me at anytime,' Finn said earnestly. 'I still think that you ought to have let me keep an eye on you at that museum! But you was always headstrong!'

'You had better show us what you have found out,' Laurence advised.

Finn, nothing loath, rose from the seat he occupied at the lowest end of the table and went out, returning a moment later with the waterproof bag in which she had placed the wooden figure.

'He has told me nothing of the progress of his labours,' Laurence said. 'Finn dislikes having an audience of one.'

'I wouldn't know, sir, not having been blessed with the thespian tendency,' Finn said. 'Mind you, I saw *Hamlet* played once years back and I figured I could've done better. Blessed actor couldn't screw himself up to kill the guilty man and ended up killing all sorts of people! So! It was a question of getting off the varnish and finding out if the figure came into two halves! It meant a lot of patient scraping. I couldn't risk burning it off and I had to buy varnish that matched exactly to recover the thing once you'd had a good look. The wood's pinewood, very plain and well seasoned but not ancient. It comes apart along the sides of the figure. It's got an extra strip of glue there to hold the two edges together. A sharp knife will see to that!'

He took out the figure where in places the old varnish had been striped and produced a sharp knife.

'Are you telling me that you haven't actually opened it yet?' Laurence expostulated.

'It was a temptation, sir,' Finn admitted, 'for there is something inside. Fits snugly too for when you tap the wood the sound's not hollow. No, I figured that if I found jewels or gold I might be tempted back into thieving ways, Mr Clark, and that is not my intention.'

'We applaud your forbearance,' Laurence said solemnly. 'Now for heaven's sake, open the thing!'

Finn, frowning in concentration, slit the glue slowly and carefully. It had hardened and lost its elasticity, the two halves of the crudely carved figure separating with little resistance.

'Done!' he pronounced at last and carefully lifted the top half of the figure.

What lay, snugly fitting the hollow within, was wrapped in oilcloth.

'You unwrap it, Finn,' Laurence said generously. 'You put in the work.'

Finn nodded and began cautiously to peel away the layers of thin yellowish material that hid what he held in his large hands.

The last thin layer drifted to the carpet and he held up the figure within, a figure that had fitted exactly into the hollow.

A queen, almost eighteen inches high, glittered between his hands. Apart from a gasp from Tansy, complete silence reigned for almost a minute.

The figure was made of gold, the features delicate, diamonds adorning the small proud head with its waterfall of gold hair, more jewels adorning the stiff golden skirt.

Finn passed it silently to Laurence, who stood it on its base on the table. Its long cloak had been fashioned from tiny amethysts, its shoes resting on the golden base were decorated with turquoise and lapis-lazuli. On the golden hands, each finger minutely detailed, were rings of diamonds echoing the head-dress.

Tansy found her voice first.

'It's beautiful,' she breathed. 'It's the most beautiful thing I've ever seen! How old?'

'Not contemporary with the biblical Vashti,' Laurence said, taking it from her. 'It would require an expert opinion to judge its date exactly, but third century AD? Certainly a unique piece, don't you think, Frank?'

'I know sufficient about antiques to fit into an eggcup,' Frank said, taking the little statue and turning it over in his hands. 'At a guess I'd say it was worth a great deal of money?'

'Probably a king's ransom,' Finn said

gloomily. 'I must say as how old ambition stirs in me when I look at it! If I'd had the chance to fence this!'

'Content yourself with rewriting *Hamlet*,' Laurence said severely. 'Tansy, you have a nose for what's genuinely antique. What do you think?'

'I'd say it must be at least fifteen hundred years old,' Tansy said, taking it back. 'It's been most carefully preserved.'

'Probably in numerous places of concealment.' Her father nodded. 'It must've passed through many hands, travelled across many countries, been sold, stolen, lost and found. A pity the lady cannot speak and tell us of her adventures.'

'This is the statuette that Carl Royston has been seeking for years,' Tansy said. 'He's had a cabinet made especially to hold it — not a glass cabinet but one of solid wood where nobody will ever see it except Carl Royston, who can gloat over it in private. Pa, he's a dreadful man!'

'Millionaires often are,' Laurence said.

11

'You really ought to have told me all this before,' Frank said. 'What's the use of working together when one of us doesn't inform the others of the full facts?'

'I really didn't want to worry anybody,' Tansy protested.

'Worry,' Finn pontificated, 'doesn't mean having to panic!'

'It seems to me,' Laurence said thoughtfully, 'that there's someone with a twisted sense of humour behind all this. Carl Royston founds a museum and then loses interest, doesn't trouble to visit or arrange for new exhibits to be delivered. Incidentally he doesn't attend any of the directors' meetings at the Kensington Museum either. He largely shuts himself away in his house and broods over his unfaithful wife and the statuette he's heard about and wants to hide away, and it's in his own museum!'

'For how long?' Tansy asked.

By common consent they all looked at Finn.

'Hard to say!' he said disappointingly. 'The case is maybe twenty years old? It's been glued and varnished in the last year or two I'd say.'

'Someone found the statuette, smuggled it over here and hid it in the last place he might expect to look. The two assistant curators might've been either involved or found out something. Fences are sometimes removed in case they give evidence. Isn't that so, Finn?'

'I can't really say,' Finn responded somewhat sheepishly. 'I always got nabbed by the police before anyone could get around to murdering me.'

'For which we are profoundly grateful,' Laurence said solemnly.

'Pa, there's something else I have to tell you,' Tansy said impulsively. 'I wasn't going to say anything because it didn't seem to have any direct bearing on present circumstances but Carl Royston told me that a rumour the statue had been smuggled to Jamaica had reached him.'

'Jamaica!' Laurence looked at her sharply. 'And?'

'He sent agents out there — twelve years ago,' she said haltingly. 'Geoffrey had just died and the agents — they opened his grave in case the statue was buried there. I didn't want to tell you. I didn't want to hear it myself. Geoffrey had nothing to do with anything!'

'He was deeply interested in antiques and quite knowledgeable about them,' Laurence said.

'Geoffrey was interested in pottery!' Tansy exclaimed. 'He knew quite a lot about it and he taught me a considerable amount too!'

'My dear daughter,' Laurence said, his tone edged with a subtle impatience, 'nobody is saying that Geoffrey had anything to do with smuggling anything, but was his the only grave opened up?'

'I believe so,' she said reluctantly.

'Then put your personal feelings aside and look at the facts! There was an outbreak of yellow fever in Kingston the year that Geoffrey went there to settle his late father's affairs. Many people died. Yet his was the only grave opened? Why?'

'As far as I know it was. Perhaps because he'd just arrived from England or because he did take an interest in antiques? I don't know, Pa! At that point I cut the interview short and left. I gave in my notice at the museum too so on Friday I get my final payment.'

'That's a pity,' Laurence said. 'Once the statuette is back in that storeroom — '

'Not just the casing?' Frank broke in.

'Sooner or later that statuette is going to be passed on to someone,' Laurence said 'If it's opened and found to be empty it will be obvious that it was taken from its hiding place in the Chelsea Museum. The only two people who could've done that are William Benson who obviously didn't and as far as I know had no reason to and Tansy here who had sole charge of the keys for one afternoon. Now Tansy has given in her notice she is more subject to any suspicion since it might well appear that, having secured the figure, she had no further interest in the place.'

'You want me to rescind my notice,' Tansy said.

'Offer to work there an extra week,' Laurence urged. 'That will effectively divert any suspicion that might fall on you though once the thing is back in its niche its absence may never have been noticed. When can you have that casing reglued and revarnished, Finn?'

'By tomorrow evening,' Finn said, 'but the meals'll be scratch ones. Varnish has to dry though I do know a trick or two to speed that up.'

'So you can get it back into the storeroom on Thursday?' Frank looked at her.

'While Mr Benson is having his lunch in the café.' She nodded.

'Suspecting nothing. Tansy, I'm sorry you had to hear about the opening of Geoffrey's grave but you must realize that it was odd that his should be the only one disturbed,' Laurence said.

'According to Carl Royston, who seems to make it his business to find out everything he can about everybody else and then hug the information to himself before he springs a surprise on the unsuspecting victim,' Tansy said bitterly.

'And Geoffrey did visit the Near East just before you got engaged,' he went on implacably. 'He paid a brief visit to Persia.'

'To help in a dig! His interest was in pottery!'

'If he'd found something so valuable wouldn't he have handed it over to the authorities?' Frank said.

'Of course he would!' Tansy cried indignantly.

'Unless he didn't know what he was carrying,' Frank said.

'Would Geoffrey have checked through his luggage carefully?' Laurence asked Tansy.

'I've no idea. I never travelled anywhere with him,' she said, casting her mind back with some difficulty. 'When he went on one of his trips he always took a large carpet-bag into which he packed his clothes and his personal necessaries and a lined trunk, small, for anything he bought in the way of souvenirs or antiques, but his trunk was always locked.'

'And the carpet-bag?' Finn asked.

'I don't think it had a lock on it,' Tansy said, frowning. 'He just put his clothes and his shaving kit in the carpet-bag. Never anything valuable!'

'He paid a brief visit to Persia and then sailed to Jamaica,' Laurence said. 'Did it not strike you as odd at the time that when your house had been bought and furnished and your wedding was due within a few months that he should make a side detour to Persia before going to Jamaica to settle his father's estate?'

'No, and it didn't strike you as unusual either,' Tansy said bluntly. 'He wanted to buy a couple of vases as an extra gift for me.'

They had arrived with the rest of his things weeks after news of his death had reached them. She recalled with painful vividness how she had felt when she had set the beautiful vases on the mantelshelf in the long sitting-room.

'If Geoffrey's effects were sent on after his death they'd go through customs clearance,' Frank said, thinking aloud. 'Wouldn't we have heard if anything had been confiscated?'

'Not all customs men are honest,' Laurence pointed out. 'Wouldn't you agree, Finn?'

'Can't rightly say, sir!' The manservant looked doubtful. 'I never fenced nothing from foreign parts. Too dangerous.'

'Geoffrey would have handed over anything as obviously rare and valuable to the correct authorities if he'd found it himself,' Tansy repeated obstinately. 'If he ever had the figure then I'm positive it was slipped into his carpet-bag. He never did fold and sort his clothes very carefully. Then he went to Jamaica and died and someone followed him and — '

'And dug in his grave,' Laurence said. 'I'm sorry you had to learn that, my dear.'

'But it was twelve years ago!' she said energetically. 'Where has it been for twelve years?'

'Passed on from hand to hand, reburied and dug up again. When people work on the wrong side of the law they must be prepared to wait sometimes for years until the initial hue and cry has died down and the stolen object can be moved,' Laurence said.

'Not in my criminal career,' Finn observed. 'Get in, grab the goods, get out quick and sell them on even quicker was my motto.'

'Which is why you were such an abject failure as a criminal,' Laurence rejoined. 'Anyway, you went for sideboard silver not priceless antiques.'

185

'I know my limits,' Finn said modestly.

'I ought to be going,' Tansy said, catching sight of the clock 'Pa, are you sure we ought not to simply hand the statue over to the legitimate authorities?'

'Normally I'd agree but putting it back in the storeroom will enhance our chances of finding who killed the two assistant curators,' her father said. 'Actually, I rather wish that you were not the one entrusted with returning it.'

'It'll be perfectly safe,' she assured him. 'I'll have it back in its hiding place by Thursday afternoon, and I'll offer to work an extra week just to help out. Mr Benson is expecting troops of school children. I cannot think why!'

'He's hoping the wish is father to the deed,' Frank said. 'Come on, Tansy. I'll take you home.'

'Thanks but I think I'll take myself home!' she retorted lightly. 'No, honestly, Frank, if you're going to hover around like a mother hen with one chick I'll regret telling you about the other incidents. Anyway, we don't really know whether or not they're connected.'

'I reckon someone started by trying to frighten you off and when that didn't work pushed you into the river,' Finn said, 'and I still wish you'd let me hang around the café just to be on the safe side!'

'If someone spots you standing guard,' Tansy said firmly, 'they'll know that I'm involved and that will draw more unwelcome attention to me. Frank, if you will call a cab for me I'll wait here in the front hall until it arrives and I won't get out until I'm at my own front door.'

'I'll see about the cab!' Finn left with an air of due importance.

'He'll tell him to wait until I'm actually inside the house,' Tansy said resignedly. 'Pa, try not to worry! I will see you tomorrow evening to collect the figure. I hope it rains on Thursday because that gives me a perfect excuse to carry a waterproof bag.'

She went down the stairs rather more lightly than she felt. The deaths of two respectable insignificant men were becoming complicated by too many side issues.

'Take care of yourself, Tansy girl!' Frank, joining her as Finn directed the oncoming cab to the nearest spot, touched her cheek gently with his forefinger and stood back as Finn opened the cab door with something of a flourish.

The drive back to Chelsea was uneventful. She was glad of the respite because questions were circling in her head which refused to be answered.

When she reached her house she noted with faint amusement that the cabbie did indeed wait until she had inserted her key in the lock and the glow of lamplight beamed through the half open door.

'It's very late, Miss Tansy,' Mrs Timothy said, coming into the hall. 'I took the liberty of sending Tilde off to her bed. She's all of a tizzy because that Robert Blake came calling bold as you like to ask her to go for a cup of tea and some cake with him on Saturday. Mind you he's a nice enough lad, and he brought over four very tender little chops and half a dozen of those herb sausages the butcher makes so well.'

'I'm sure Tilde will be safe with him.' Tansy said, straight-faced. 'You get off to bed now! I'll check the locks again though I'm sure you've already done so. I intend to sit up and read for a spell.'

The fire had been damped down in the sitting-room but the coals still glowed comfortably when she stirred them with a poker.

She eased off her shoes and sat down, reaching for the book that lay on the side table, but she felt too restless to concentrate on the rather anodyne love story contained within its pages. She could think only of the statue with its jewels glittering in the lamplight and the small beautifully chiselled features of the golden face and the hands holding out the sides of the stiff golden skirt. Craftsmen who could create a thing of such exquisite perfection were rare indeed in this Victorian world, with its draped sofas and ornate vases and heavily embossed dinner services. Geoffrey had taught her to appreciate cleaner, simpler lines, to turn her back on what was false and fussy and overdecorated.

It was no use! She needed to walk and sort out the questions thronging in her brain. She bent to put on her shoes again, reached for a scarf to tie over her head in place of hat or bonnet and pistol snugly tucked in her pocket, unlocked the French window and stepped out on to the terrace, carefully shutting the glass doors behind her. She had no intention of straying very far since her father's and Frank's concern must be taken seriously and for her own part she felt an unwanted nervousness as she walked slowly down the garden towards the low wall that separated it from the river-bank.

In the garden the moon's white radiance bleached the branches of the trees and haloed the surrounding bushes, some already denuded of leaves and blossoms, others displaying the first greening holly berries and the tips of yellowing leaves. On the breeze hung the damp sour-sweet scents of autumn.

Almost without thinking she stepped over the low wall and turned to the left, slackening her pace, conscious of the gentle murmuring of the water, the ripples as the sleek head of a water rat broke the surface. Much further down river she heard the long hollow boom of a ship making its way to harbour.

Her previous troubled thoughts were lulled by the murmuring of river and breeze and by the Jacob's-ladder that stretched to the further side of the water, seeming as it moved to keep pace with herself like some unbidden but welcome companion.

At intervals the grass was interrupted by patches of cobblestone that gleamed darkly. Sir Thomas More had lived here in this part of London, she recalled, and been Chancellor to Henry VIII until he had objected to the latter's marriage to Anne Boleyn and resigned the Great Seal and ended, she reminded herself, under the executioner's axe on Tower Hill. There had been graft and corruption in those days too and women had loved and lost . . .

Half-turning her head to follow the rays of the moon as it drifted gently behind a cloud, she sensed rather than saw the shadow flitting silently between two trees away to her left. Somebody was following her then. Robert

Blake hadn't been mistaken.

She felt a tensing of her muscles as her hand tightened on the pistol in her pocket and her heartbeat sounded loud in her ears, mingling with the wash of the tide and the creaking of boughs as the trees strained against the night.

She had almost reached the little wooden bridge. Stepping on to the rough planks she drew a long shivering breath and turned, pistol in hand.

The figure approaching wore a long overcoat, its fur collar almost concealing the lower part of the face. For an instant it stood motionless no more than few feet away.

'Hello, Tansy.'

The whisper chilled her blood.

'This pistol is loaded.'

With surprise she heard the calm tenor of her own voice almost as if another calmer person had replied.

'I hope you're not thinking of shooting me!' Geoffrey said.

The voice hadn't changed. It had echoed through her years of mourning.

She could feel herself whirling through darkness. Then something stronger than panic banished the faintness and she heard herself say, 'You didn't die after all. You didn't die!'

12

At that instant she felt herself whirling backward through the years, experienced a sense of déjà vu so strongly that she looked at the pistol in her hand with a sense of astonishment, for a brief flash in time uncertain why she was holding it or what she was doing on the river-bank in the middle of the night anyway.

'You really ought to take your finger off the trigger,' Geoffrey said.

She did so automatically, slipping the weapon back into her pocket but keeping a secure hold of it as if it represented safety in an unfamiliar world.

'You're not going to faint on me either, are you?' Geoffrey said.

'I'm not the fainting type,' Tansy found voice to say.

'The perfect daughter for a police inspector! I wish the moonlight was stronger so that I could look at you properly. My instincts tell me that the years have made you even more lovely.'

'I was never lovely in the first place,' Tansy said in a small, hard voice.

Somehow the lilt of his caressing voice had grated on her ear. Almost with a sense of the inevitable she felt him draw her arm through his and turn to walk slowly towards a solitary lamp that illuminated some nets strung out to dry.

Seeing him more clearly now, as he folded down the concealing collar she knew him at once. He had scarcely altered in twelve years save to have gained a little weight.

'Who lies in your grave?' she heard herself say.

'One of the estate workers had died of the fever the previous day. He was an itinerant worker whom nobody would miss and of course when yellow fever runs through the community coffins are quickly sealed. I stayed out of sight and he was buried in my stead.'

'But why? Why did you — '

'I had a valuable piece.' He released her from his grasp and leaned against a tree that spanned the footbridge. 'It was a figure of great antiquity. She would have made my fortune!'

'But you had inherited your father's estate — '

'Which left me very comfortably off but to be rich beyond the dreams of avarice! Think of it, Tansy. More money than either of us had ever dreamed about! Others wanted it too. Others believed that I still possessed it.'

'You didn't have it?' she said in confusion.

He shook his head.

'I had a partner. I trusted him implicitly.' He sounded aggrieved. 'He stole the figure and vanished. He was never a friend. However, he had the gift of ferreting out some of the rarest antiquities in the world.'

'You were a thief,' she said flatly.

'I stole nothing, Tansy. I merely relied on my associate to keep me informed when some piece he knew would interest me became known. He passed on such information and saw to the practical details of our arrangement.'

'But you didn't need the money!'

'My father's estate in Jamaica was a fairly modest one. Oh, it provided a comfortable lifestyle but not wealth beyond our dreams — '

'Don't couple my dreams with yours!' she said sharply. Inside her, cold anger was building up, layer by layer.

'The problem,' he said, shifting his position slightly, 'was that others believed I had the piece in question since it wouldn't have been in my interest to reveal my connections with the one who had made off with it. So I was forced to disappear completely and the outbreak of yellow fever rendered everything more convenient.'

'You disappeared for twelve years!' she burst out. 'Twelve years, Geoffrey! Where have you been?'

'Mainly in South America. I even tried my hand at ranching, but always I kept track of the figure. It's a second- or third-century piece representing Queen Vashti out of the Bible. The figure's of gold and the jewels! Tansy, they would make your mouth water!'

He didn't know that she had found the piece then, she thought, trying to marshal her defences, else he would never have described it to her.

Her sense of shock was diminishing slightly and anger was rising to take its place. Now above all times she needed to keep a check on her feelings, she told herself severely.

'We were going to be married,' she heard herself saying in a bewildered voice. 'You could have written to me, let me know by some means, not left me to believe — '

'It was safer for you to believe that I'd died out in Jamaica,' he said, 'and you weren't exactly left impoverished, now, were you? Incidentally, the house, your income, they come from the legitimate proceeds of the sale of my father's estate — plantation they call it over there though it never was as grand as that sounds. So you can go on enjoying it with a clear conscience because those profits, though more modest than I hoped they would be, were honestly won.'

'Why have you come back?' Tansy asked abruptly.

'Because we were going to be married. Because you have always been in my mind.'

'Liar!' She flung the word at him with such bitterness that she saw him recoil. 'Liar! You don't even know the meaning of the word love! You let me believe you were dead! Did you really think that a nice house and a comfortable income made up for all the shock and the grief? And why have you returned now? Why, Geoffrey? Because after twelve years you've realized that you still love me passionately — though I seem to recall passion never entered much into our relationship!'

She was walking on rapidly, wanting only to distance herself from the man she had mourned for so long, the man who had perhaps only existed in her own mind.

'Tansy, wait!' His hand was on her shoulder and she twisted away furiously.

'Don't touch me, Geoffrey! Don't pretend an emotion you've probably never really felt in your life! Why are you here?'

'Because I know where my old partner is,' he said, his arm dropping to his side. 'I am

196

certain he still has the figure. There have been rumours for years but rumours without evidence are worth very little. Of course I told you nothing during our engagement!'

'You told me nothing because you knew how I would feel if I learned that if our innocent trips to look at pottery in various museums were simply a cover for your real activities — stealing valuable antiques from other countries and selling them off by dubious means!'

'And if I had told you,' he rejoined, 'would you have understood my point of view? Would you have fled with me to South America and waited there for the time when the rumours about the stolen Vashti began to surface again? Your father was a police officer and you yourself limited by your own respectability!'

'But you're here now,' she said.

'Yes, I'm here now,' he said. There was an underlying sadness in his voice against which she steeled herself.

'Because you thought your former partner might be here? And while you were waiting for him to turn up you decided to amuse yourself first by following your former fiancée — namely myself — and then deciding it wasn't worth renewing my acquaintance and shoving me into the river instead! A neat way of disposing of someone who might identify you!'

'Tansy, what the devil are you talking about?' he broke in.

'Oh, don't pretend!' she exclaimed, too angry to be nervous. 'You followed me and — '

'That's true,' he interrupted. 'I guessed that you would have moved into our house, the one we planned together, but I wondered if you'd married in the meantime, if you had a family. Now and then I'd managed to get hold of an English newspaper and I always scanned it carefully but I never saw anything about you. Then I returned here and, yes, I took cheap lodgings in another part of town but I did come here into Chelsea. You've a young girl working for you.'

'Tilde. She knew she'd been followed. I knew I'd been followed too but I could find no signs that my instinct had been correct.'

'I wanted to make myself known to you but I didn't want to startle you — '

'Very considerate! So you decided to push — '

'I pushed nobody into any river anywhere!' Geoffrey sounded highly indignant but whether that was genuine or feigned she couldn't tell. More and more she was beginning to feel that this was a man she had never really known at all.

'You entered my house,' she said dully.

'I could hardly startle you out of your wits by ringing the front door bell,' he said. 'I climbed up into the bedroom — you ought to lock your windows, by the bye — and was on my way down the stairs when that girl — '

'Tilde.'

'Tilde came out into the hall and asked if I — that's to say you — wanted anything. I had the wit to turn and start back up the stairs when I heard her footsteps — '

'And you were wearing cloak and hood,' Tansy said bitterly. 'Does it amuse you to put on disguises?'

'Cloaks and hoods are fairly anonymous. Sometimes it's useful to be anonymous.'

'You'll be delivering presents at Christmas time next,' she gibed. Her shock and initial terror had evaporated and she felt only weary disillusion.

'When she returned into kitchen I came down the stairs again, let myself out quietly via the French windows and left the glove on the floor. I hoped that you with your quick intuition would connect the incident with me and not be so shocked when I made myself known to you.'

'How considerate! Well, you overestimated my intuition. I was completely bewildered by the whole incident and Mrs Timothy and Tilde were very much alarmed. Have you any more pretty little tricks up your sleeve, Geoffrey?'

'You've had a bad shock,' he said, sounding she thought angrily, as if he was humouring a child.

They had been proceeding slowly along the bank and stood now by the low wall that separated it from her long back garden.

'Oh, twelve years has toughened me up amazingly,' she said. 'Twelve years can change a person, you know.'

'But surely not a person's feelings? Tansy, you don't know how often I took pen and paper and started to write to you, to beg you to join me or at the least to forgive my deception.'

'I'm tired, Geoffrey, and it's very late,' she said coldly. 'I take it that you don't want your resurrection announced to anyone?'

'I know I can rely on your absolute discretion,' he said. 'But now that we're reunited you can help me. Any stray piece of information about a priceless statue — '

'I have no such information!'

'But you're working at the Royston Museum. Why would you be going out to work unless — '

'Your years in South America have addled

your wits,' Tansy said. 'I don't need to work but I do quite a lot of collecting for charity and your example has at least interested me in antiques. I took the job simply for a change. Nothing more!'

'But if you were to hear anything.'

'I would inform the proper authorities. You came to seek your erstwhile partner who has, it seems, cheated you. Devote your energies to that and leave me out of your life in future.'

'There has to be something left of the feelings we once had,' he protested.

'Only the most profound thankfulness that we never married,' she said. 'Goodbye, Geoffrey.' Stepping over the wall, evading his reaching hand, she walked rapidly up the narrow path on to the terrace. When she glanced back very briefly as she let herself in through the French windows, she saw that he was still standing there, bulky in his overcoat, but she felt no inclination to acknowledge his continuing presence.

She had loved him and gone on loving him because death couldn't kill love but deception and greed could.

Bolting the doors behind her and drawing the long curtains across, she sat down and tried to poke the glowing ashes into their previous blaze but there were only a few spurts of flame before they blackened and fell away.

What she ought to do, she decided, suddenly feeling an immense weariness, was to check all the locks again and then go to bed. For the moment she resolved to say nothing about Geoffrey's reappearance. Her first task must be to collect the figure from her father and return it to the museum on Thursday morning. Or was it?

Closing her bedroom door and checking that the window was also securely fastened, she sat down on the edge of her bed and pondered the matter.

Geoffrey had returned for the statue provided he could locate it and also to wreak some kind of revenge upon a partner who had double-crossed him. She had roused his suspicions by working in the Royston Museum in the first place and it was likely that he'd be keeping a watch on her activities. If he saw her with a large waterproof bag going into the museum he might well jump to the right conclusion and steal the figure back again. On the other hand she didn't want to alarm her father by relating the meeting with Geoffrey until it became absolutely necessary. Laurence Clark might be retired and enjoy using his wits in an unofficial capacity but he would certainly revert to being the conscientious police officer once he had this new information in his possession.

Suddenly she was overwhelmed by such tiredness that she could only just manage to slip off her shoes before she lay down, pulled the covers over her and sank, fully dressed, into a deep and satisfying sleep.

★　★　★

Morning woke her before Tilde's knock on the door. She felt rested but not refreshed and a look in the mirror told her bluntly she looked every day of her thirty-five years.

Fortunately there were as yet only faint sounds from below. She was able to strip off her clothes and take a bath and try, though not altogether successfully, to wash away the memory of the previous night before Tilde tapped at her door with the customary tray.

'You look tired, Miss Tansy!' she observed, surveying her mistress with a critical and caring eye. 'Mrs Timothy is of the opinion that if you keep at this museum work much longer you'll do in your back!'

'My brains more likely,' Tansy said with somewhat weary humour. 'Well, you may tell Mrs Timothy that I've decided to give up the job though I may work one more week there until a replacement is hired.'

'She'll be very pleased to hear it,' Tilde assured her. 'Oh, and Miss Tansy, that nice young man I was telling you about — '

'Robert Blake, the butcher's son, yes?'

'Cake and coffee on Saturday evening,' Tilde said. 'Mrs Timothy quite approves.'

'I thought she might,' Tansy said.

'And I think you might have an admirer too,' the girl chatted on.

'Frank Cartwright is a close friend — '

'No, miss, not Frank Cartwright,' Tilde said. 'There's been a gentleman walking up and down for quite a long time already this morning outside the house.'

'What sort of gentleman?' Tansy asked sharply.

'Well, I've not seen his face clearly because he has his collar up but he's pacing up and down,' Tilde said.

'Forget pacing gentlemen and go and help get breakfast on the table,' Tansy said.

Geoffrey, she thought, obviously meant to be persistent in what she was supposed to think was his renewed courtship of her but Tansy knew only too clearly that the long-lost fiancé had other matters on his mind beside love.

By the time she had eaten her breakfast and put on her outdoor garments, the street was empty. She stepped out briskly and walked rapidly to the museum without slowing her step to look round.

As she had expected there was no sign of the threatened influx of school children and she spent the morning sweeping the floors, Mr Benson being concerned lest the always-awaited public would be shocked by what had collected in the corners of the silent, uninspiring rooms.

Her own mind was still absorbing the shock of Geoffrey's sudden reappearance. What she had somewhat hastily already decided was that she couldn't inform her father or Frank what had happened. Geoffrey, no matter how one chose to look at it, was a smuggler of stolen antiquities with, it seemed, a most unreliable partner. Geoffrey was also the fiancé she had mourned through twelve long years. Laurence would, if told of the latest developments, insist on justice being done, which meant he would be forced to assist in the arrest of the man his daughter had loved.

For the moment at least, she would keep news of the latest events to herself and simply make an excuse to delay the return of the statue to prevent Geoffrey from getting his hands on it.

When she went across to the café to drink some strong coffee and nibble on a roll and butter in a half-hearted way that would have horrified Mrs Timothy and Tilde, the exhaustion of the previous night had given way to a settled weariness, as if not only her physical strength but her mental energies had been drained.

'Tansy? Might we have a word?' With no great sense of surprise she looked up as Geoffrey took the chair opposite to her.

'The last thing I want at the moment,' she said coldly, 'is a word with you.'

'I startled you greatly last night,' he said apologetically. 'The truth is that I was as nervous as you. How can one calmly walk back into someone's life after being presumed dead for so many years?'

'You seem to have coped quite adequately,' Tansy said.

'But not without nerving myself up for the event.'

'Having already broken into my house to leave a hint of your continued survival! I'm sorry, Geoffrey, but you and I have nothing now in common, and if you hadn't learned that I had a job at Royston's museum I doubt if you'd've taken any interest in me or how I was at all!'

'I missed you,' he said.

'But pretending to be dead so that you could eventually track down your partner and wait for news of the missing statue meant more to you than a mere wedding to the woman you were supposed to love!'

'I did love you, Tansy. There's been nobody since whom I would consider marrying.'

'If that's meant as a compliment,' she said icily, 'it falls far short of the mark. Geoffrey, the plain fact is that it's over. I loved you and then I lost you and now I realize that I don't love you at all. In fact I've been loving the memory of something that never really existed.'

'I still exist!'

'Yes.' She looked across the table at him, seeing the face she had held in memory for so long, a little coarser now, the hair thinning slightly at the temples. It had no power to stir any emotion in her at all.

'We have to talk,' he was saying, his voice persuasive. 'It's been twelve years — '

'Since you went off to Jamaica, fitting in a brief visit to Persia on the way. When the figure came into your hands, returning to marry me must have seemed tame indeed!'

'The figure was stolen!'

'And instead of marking that down to bad luck and getting on with the rest of your life — our lives — you chose to fake your death and go after what wasn't yours in the first place!'

'There were those who believed that I still held it,' he protested. 'There are ruthless men behind all this.'

'Oh, you did it to protect me?' She kept her voice low but her green eyes blazed. 'No, I'll not bear that burden for the sake of your peace of mind! You knew that I'd have no truck with stolen property and neither would Pa! So you decided that the happiness of marriage wasn't worth the excitement of looking for the figure again and seeking out the partner who double-crossed you, and being 'dead' protected you from those who were seeking you in the belief that you still held it. That's the plain truth, isn't it?'

'Is everything all right, miss?' The waitress had approached, her expression one of concern.

'Quite all right,' Tansy said crisply. 'This gentleman was only enquiring the way somewhere but I just told him the road was closed some years ago.'

Geoffrey had risen and she wondered suddenly if he was going to lose his temper, not something she could ever recall him doing, but he merely gave her a stiff little bow and left the café. Tansy, sipping her cooling coffee, was annoyed to find she was trembling slightly but it was reaction and not fear or grief. The grief, she acknowledged, had died along with the person she had believed Geoffrey to be.

She paid her bill and walked soberly back to the museum.

'Is everything all right, Miss Clark?' William Benson bestirred himself as she came through the door.

'I believe I am a little tired,' she confessed.

'If you wish to leave a few minutes before time then you may do so,' he said almost graciously, nodding his head at her.

'I didn't sleep well last night,' she excused herself. 'However, tomorrow I will stay on a little longer.'

'You display a neat sense of priorities, Miss Clark,' he approved. 'The young are so often remiss in that respect. I shall be sorry to lose you next week.'

Unwilling to commit herself, she made some indeterminate reply, gave Antonio a wink as she passed by him to collect her toilet bag from the little room designated for her convenience, and set off for home.

She was barely out of sight of the museum when heavy footsteps behind caused her to turn.

'Finn, you promised not to — ' she began crossly.

'I'm sorry, Miss Tansy, but your pa and I got to talking last night after you and Mr

Frank had left and we simply don't like the notion of you marching into that museum with the figure in your bag,' Finn said. 'It's asking for trouble. Your pa thinks that it ought to stay with us for a few days and be handed over to the right authorities as soon as possible. And your pa and I don't think that you ought to work an extra week at that place either. You've given in your notice so you can just walk away on Friday. That's what your pa and I think and when I next see Mr Frank he'll agree with us. So it's no use arguing because — '

'I wasn't going to argue,' Tansy said. 'I was coming to the same opinion myself.'

'Your pa will be pleased to hear that,' Finn said in some surprise.

'Tell Pa that I won't come over this evening,' she told him. 'I need to sort out some affairs of my own.'

'Yes, Miss Tansy.' Finn would, she guessed, have loved to offer some more advice but he merely patted her arm and went off.

'There's some lovely flowers come for you, Miss Tansy,' Tilde said when she opened the door as Tansy walked up the front path. 'Orchids! Little striped orchids and no note or anything. I don't think Mr Frank left them at the door and went off without ringing the bell. I think you've got a secret admirer!'

'Where are they?' Tansy asked.

'I put them in those two vases you have on the mantelpiece,' Tilde said. 'They look ever so French!'

'Most orchids come from South America,' Tansy said, going into the long sitting-room. What she wanted to do was pull them out of the vases and fling them on the fire but that would have been childish and upset her maid, who had arranged them with great care and a certain flair for the artistic. Instead she conjured up a smile, said a few complimentary words and headed upstairs to her bedroom.

Seated on the edge of the bed, she looked about her at the tasteful, beautifully kept furnishings and furniture. She and Geoffrey had enjoyed choosing and buying everything for their future home. Yet he had been already involved in the smuggling of illegal antiquities. Had he given more than a passing thought to the possibility that one day he might be caught, tried, sentenced? He had, she supposed, already provided for her in his will, not then knowing he would be forced to feign death.

He had loved her in his own fashion, she thought wearily, but there had been no passion in it, and when occasion informed against him he already had the necessary arrangements in place without considering that other people could suffer heartbreak.

She reached to the bedside table and opened the top drawer. Geoffrey's photograph lay there. Once it had occupied a frame on the bedside table where she could see it, even talk to it in her imagination.

She took out the photograph and a sharp pair of nail scissors and neatly, painstakingly, cut the photograph into shreds, then moving to the fire that Tilde had lit against the chill of the day she fed the pieces one by one to the hungry little flames and felt nothing more than an immense relief when the task was done.

13

The morning brought a chill wind that twisted the bushes into alien shapes and blew stray wisps of Tansy's hair from their confining snood. She had donned her plainest grey outfit since there was rain on the wind and carried her umbrella, thinking as she walked to the museum that nobody throwing her a casual glance would mistake her for anything more than a respectable spinster on her way somewhere or other.

At least she didn't have to worry about smuggling the figure back into the storeroom! Her father would contact the authorities who might or might not connect the finding of the figure with the deaths of the two assistant curators. She doubted whether Laurence would mention the fact. Since his immobilization in a wheelchair he had greatly relished presenting his erstwhile colleagues with solutions nicely proved.

'Tansy!'

She knew who it was almost before she heard the voice and turned abruptly.

'What do you want, Geoffrey?' There was no need to feign coldness.

'I behaved badly,' he said, coming to her side.

'You dealt in stolen antiques and when the disappearance of the Vashti statue and the betrayal of your so-called partner made things dangerous for you, you faked your own death and hied off to South America leaving me to grieve for the fiancé I had trusted implicitly? Yes, I would agree that you behaved rather badly, Geoffrey!' she said bitingly.

'I had already willed the house we chose together to you and all the legitimate profits from the sale of my late father's plantation,' he protested.

'That was very noble of you!' she jeered.

'And I still have most loving feelings for you,' he continued.

'The river?'

'Tansy, for God's sake! Give me a little credit! I'm not a violent man. I've never killed anyone in my life and whoever pushed you into the river, it wasn't me! Why would anyone do that anyway? You're not helping your father with anything at the moment, are you?'

'I'm merely helping out at the Royston Museum,' she told him. 'I get bored sometimes with collecting for charity, you know.'

'We never went there together, did we? I

believe it has nothing of interest.'

'Nothing,' she said levelly. 'I leave tomorrow and charity collecting is going to seem vastly more interesting in comparison!'

'You don't think that you and I — '

'There is no you and I any longer, Geoffrey,' she said. 'If you are in danger from people who believe you have this statue then surely you would be better advised to sail back to South America on the first available ship and hope that one day your treacherous partner arrives there and makes his apologies.'

'But the Vashti figure may be here in London!'

'Then you look for it if you like. I have a steadily decreasing interest in anything more than fifteen years old.'

'I left flowers, Tansy!' He gave her an appealing, little-boy look designed to melt the hardest heart.

'Flowers wither and feelings die,' she returned briskly. 'Goodbye, Geoffrey.'

Walking on towards the museum, she resisted the small temptation to turn her head and see if he was still standing there.

'You're four minutes late, Miss Clark,' William Benson accused as she entered the museum.

'I was slightly delayed on the way here. The

traffic . . . ' she said vaguely.

'Ah! Traffic in London has always been chaotic,' he said. 'In the fifteenth and sixteenth centuries people used the river much more frequently which took the strain off the roads. Of course, one had to wait often for the tide to turn but how much more pleasant to move about on water than on land! However, we cannot stand gossiping here all morning! I noticed some smears on one or two of the cases. The public . . . '

She was strongly tempted to retort 'What public?' but merely nodded as if she could see droves of people waiting for admittance.

'I'll see to it at once, Mr Benson,' she said meekly and went off to fetch her dusters.

To her surprise there was a thin trickle of visitors throughout the day. Several school children did indeed arrive and were spectacularly uninterested in everything their teacher pointed out, except for one small boy who regarded Antonio gravely and said he looked sad.

'His head's not on properly, miss,' he said.

'Of course it is,' Tansy said smilingly.

'No, Miss,' the child insisted. 'It's at the wrong angle. If he stood like that on duty he'd get into a lot of trouble.'

'He's not on duty,' Tansy said firmly. 'He's waiting to go on duty!'

'And he's holding his sword all wrong,' the boy went on.

'I'll talk to him about it,' Tansy promised and escaped briefly into the hall where a woman with a small dog was protesting volubly that she would keep him firmly on the lead if he was allowed in.

All in all it was becoming quite a busy day, Tansy considered. At least it afforded her no time in which to think about Geoffrey's renewed courtship.

When she went over to the café on Mr Benson's return from his own lunch, she half expected to find Geoffrey sitting there but instead Finn looked up from the table where she habitually sat.

'Finn, I thought I told you — ' she began in exasperation.

'I know, Miss Tansy!' He rose and pulled out her chair. 'Fact is that your pa is fretting about you though he never says much.'

'The Vashti figure?' she queried in a low voice as she took her seat and Finn resumed his.

'Your pa is contacting the authorities today, Miss Tansy. He wants the little lady safe in police or customs and excise custody as quickly as possible. Seems the sooner that's done and made generally known the safer you'll be. Don't have the pork pie, miss!

Looks a bit elderly to me.'

'Soup and a roll, please,' Tansy instructed the waitress. 'Finn?'

'Eggs and bacon and toast,' Finn said. 'They won't measure up to mine but a body gets a mite peckish when he's on duty so to speak!'

'Guard duty?' Tansy shot him an irritated look. 'For heaven's sake, Finn, I'm not in any danger now!'

'Ah, that's where you're wrong, Miss Tansy,' he said, shaking his head. 'Until it's public knowledge the statue's in police custody there'll be those looking for it. There's something else you ought to know but it's likely to be a very great shock to you and though you're not the fainting kind of female — '

'Geoffrey's alive and back in London.'

'You know already?' Finn gasped at her.

Tansy nodded.

'He was the one who made what he regarded as a romantic gesture and climbed into my bedroom, took one of the gloves he once gave me and left through the French windows,' she said. 'He swears he didn't push me into the river though and I'm inclined to believe him.'

'You don't sound as if his coming back has bucked up your spirits,' Finn said.

'Geoffrey happens to be one of those who has been trying to get his hands on the Vashti figure,' Tansy told him. 'He and a partner had it for a short time and then, according to Geoffrey, the partner double-crossed him and since some very dangerous individuals believed Geoffrey still had the figure he faked his own death and went off to South America. He's back in London in the hope of regaining the statue.'

'And climbed into your bedroom for old times' sake?' Finn looked sceptical.

'Something like that. He claims that he hid away for twelve years to protect me and now — '

'You're not thinking of marrying him, Miss Tansy? Not after he kept you in mourning for twelve years!'

'No, Finn, I'm not thinking of marrying him,' Tansy said. 'I'm not thinking of marrying any person anywhere at any time! I shall work my day at the museum tomorrow and by next week I'll be collecting for charity again and arranging a treat for Tilde's twenty-first birthday. I rather think Geoffrey will leave London — leave England — as soon as the authorities announce that the figure is in official hands and I don't expect to hear of him or from him ever again!'

'He was hanging round outside your pa's place,' Finn said, 'but when he saw that I recognized him he made off fast. Your pa decided not to tell you. Thought you had enough on your plate without a dead fiancé turning up.'

'Which was precisely the reason I said nothing to you or Pa.' Tansy told him. 'Does Frank know?'

'Mr Frank knows,' Finn said. 'Your pa thought it only fair.'

'And?'

'Mr Frank took it very calm,' Finn said approvingly. 'Said you probably needed time to think things over.'

And Frank, Tansy thought, had the enchanting Susan Harris to console him for any heartache he might have experienced on hearing of Geoffrey's return.

'So that's that!' Finn said, finishing his last bit of bacon and taking a draught of his tea. 'I'll tell your pa what you told me. He'll be glad you're not upset. He was thinking of telling you himself, of course, but I said to leave it to me on account of I flatter myself I can put things more tactful.'

'Tactful? Yes, of course, Finn.'

'And I'd not be too quick if I was you, Miss Tansy, to go crying off men for life,' Finn advised. 'I ain't given up hopes of being best man at a wedding yet!'

'With which tactful remark he departed,' Tansy murmured to herself as he paid both bills and took himself off.

'Three minutes late, Miss Clark,' Mr Benson admonished when she entered the museum. 'I do hope this tardiness isn't getting to be a habit?'

'Hardly, Mr Benson, since I leave tomorrow,' Tansy said.

'And in many ways I will be sorry to lose you, Miss Clark,' he said relentingly. 'It has quite cheered up the place to have a young fresh face about. Not that Mr Fanshaw was exactly elderly — a most conscientious young man and eminently respectable.'

He had evidently not read anything yet in the newspapers about the two murder enquiries. Tansy felt convinced that Mr Benson probably confined his reading to brochures and the occasional arts magazine that might come his way.

'Are we expecting any visitors this afternoon?' she enquired, trying to keep the slight note of sarcasm out of her voice.

'I don't believe so. Why?'

'I thought I might do a bit of dusting,' Tansy said, straight-faced.

'Yes, indeed. Dust is always with us.' He looked gratified.

'The schoolchildren seemed quite interested in the exhibits,' she said kindly. 'There
was one particularly obstreperous little boy
who kept insisting that Antonio — I mean the
figure of the Roman centurion — had been
put together all wrong! I felt like slapping
him.'

'I'm relieved that you restrained yourself,
Miss Clark,' Mr Benson said with a rare
gleam of humour. 'Fortunately the blame, if
blame there be, lies neither at your door nor
mine. All the exhibits were in place when I
was offered the post of curator. Mr Royston
chose them and saw to their arrangement
personally.'

'I see,' Tansy nodded as she went to find a
clean duster.

In actual fact she felt more confused than
ever. Her visits to the Royston mansion had
shown her plainly that its owner was a
wealthy man of impeccable taste. She recalled
the exquisite ornaments in the huge salon,
the wonderfully woven rugs, the polished
floors and the sweep of the staircase. Yet Carl
Royston, a millionaire with excellent taste,
had opened a museum and filled it with the
most uninteresting objects he could have
found. Even the few exciting ones had been
hidden away behind others less interesting.
Why? Why would he found a museum and

then do everything in his power to put off the visiting public?

She had begun to polish the glass that encased Antonio and suddenly, impulsively, she heard herself saying, 'I wonder if anything new has been added to this place since it was opened.'

'Only one or two things,' Mr Benson said, having just entered the room. 'That carved seat over there and the medieval table in the next room were brought in about five years ago. They are late medieval and Mr Royston originally purchased them for his own residence and then altered his mind and donated them to the museum here. It was one of the rare occasions on which he visited the museum.'

'How on earth did they get them through the doors?' Tansy marvelled, staring at the two massive pieces of furniture.

'They were brought into the yard and hoisted up into the storeroom overhead,' he told her. 'The windows up there are very large and the actual staircase leading to the ground floor here has banisters that are removable. I believe I mentioned that new acquisitions were delivered in that manner.'

'That must have made a change in your routine,' Tansy said.

'Oh, indeed it did!' he agreed. 'As a rule,

anything delivered arrives on a Saturday when the museum is closed and I am not here, but on this occasion Mr Royston requested my presence.'

'And at other times exhibits have been delivered during your absence?'

'A pair of Portland vases which were brought in through the front door and some large carpets which you may have seen on the passage walls — nothing else.'

'Did the late assistant curator, Mr Fanshaw, ever come in on a Saturday?' Tansy pressed.

'Mr Fanshaw?' The other looked puzzled. 'Joseph Fanshaw had no keys. He worked slightly longer hours than you do but I always open and close the museum.'

'Except on Saturdays?'

'Oh, Mr Royston has keys, of course,' Mr Benson said. 'At least I assume he has keys. Since his interest and involvement in the museum is at best minimal then it's possible he has placed them in some cabinet or other and forgotten about them. However he was present when the medieval table and bench were brought in and also the carpets — the latter were brought through the front door. I was present to greet Mr Royston and Mr Fanshaw — '

'Your assistant curator was here too?' Tansy

said in some surprise.

'Yes. Mr Fanshaw expressed some interest in the expected delivery and I told him to come in. He was a very pleasant young man.'

He sighed slightly as he spoke, as if regretting the substitution of a pleasant and quiet young man for a woman who clearly knew nothing much about antiques but who spoke of them in a rather frivolous fashion, even chatting to the figure of a centurion whose head wasn't on quite correctly.

'And he died,' Tansy said.

'Yes, indeed.' For an instant there was a flash of real grief in the dried-up elderly visage.

'Perhaps you haven't yet read the newspapers this week?' Tansy began.

'I never read current newspapers,' Mr Benson said. 'Modern life I find crude and devoid of charm, and the newspapers reflect that tendency only too expertly. It probably amounts to burying my head in the sand but I prefer not to read in lavish detail about the manners and morals of the present generation.'

'Oh dear!' Tansy said involuntarily.

'Miss Clark,' he hastened to say, 'Under no circumstances would I regard your own conduct as even verging on the reprehensible!'

'Thank you,' Tansy said meekly.

'But we waste time gossiping!' he said. 'Closing time draws near and the exhibits are not in pristine condition for tomorrow's visitors.'

'My last day,' Tansy said.

'Yes, indeed.'

'Mr Benson, as you never read newspapers then you don't know that there have been recent developments in the matter of Mr Fanshaw and Mr Brook Wilton,' she said on impulse.

'Mr Brook — ? Ah yes, the assistant curator at the Kensington Museum,' he nodded. 'I don't believe I ever met the gentleman.'

'Mr Benson, both bodies have been exhumed — '

'The authorities suspect an outbreak of a more virulent disease? We have been blessedly free of cholera during this past summer.'

'Antimony,' Tansy said. 'Both men died of antimony poisoning. The symptoms resemble the symptoms of gastric fever.'

'Antimony? I have heard of it but I don't understand . . . ' He was staring at her in bewilderment.

'Mr Royston must have read about it. He hasn't informed you?'

'Mr Royston and I scarcely ever have even the most fleeting contact,' Mr Benson said.

'Miss Clark, are you certain about this? Often newspaper reporters exaggerate for the sake of sensation in order to attract more readers. Are you positive you didn't misread — ?'

'It isn't front-page news,' Tansy said. 'Both gentlemen were unknown and not, it seems, acquainted with each other, but the item definitely appeared.'

'I cannot imagine Mr Fanshaw making away with himself,' Mr Benson said. 'Granted he was alone in the world but he always appeared quietly cheerful.'

'It's a murder enquiry,' Tansy said.

'Murder! Murder connected with two most respectable museums? Oh, Miss Clark, I hope that you are mistaken.'

He couldn't have looked more horrified had she informed him that someone had stolen Antonio.

14

'So Geoffrey returned?'

Laurence Clark sipped his after-dinner brandy and shot a keen look across the table at his daughter.

'You never suspected that he might not be dead?' Tansy queried.

'Not for an instant! Why should I? You met during a visit to a museum undertaken separately by two unattached people and fell into conversation. The few enquiries I made — '

'Pa!' she interjected indignantly.

'My dear girl, you were in your early twenties and since your mother's death you had devoted yourself to me and put your own life on hold,' he said impatiently. 'I was eager for you to find a suitor and Geoffrey seemed ideal. The little he told me about his life all checked out. Born in Jamaica of English parents, mother died while he was at boarding school in England (his grades, incidentally, were always excellent), a respectable university degree in Art Research and Classics, various journeyings with published articles to supplement his allowance from his father, polite, pleasant, good-looking — he struck me as exactly the kind of young man with whom you could be happy. Had there been any breath of a suspicion against him I would have made it my business to investigate further but there was nothing. I investigate where there is some suspicion, my love, but I never claimed to be a psychic!'

'And if you'd found out anything,' Tansy said, 'I probably wouldn't have listened.'

'And now?' He favoured her with another piercing glance. 'How do you feel now?'

'I don't feel anything at all,' Tansy said, somewhat surprised at her own reply. 'No, it's true, Pa! At first when I saw him, when he spoke to me, yes, I did feel something but it fled the moment he started explaining why he had faked his own death and left me unaware for all those years.'

'Having provided quite handsomely for you,' Laurence reminded her.

'He thought a house and an income equalled loving.'

'Have you spoken to Frank yet?'

'I haven't seen him since we discovered the statue of Vashti,' Tansy said lightly. 'No doubt he's squiring Miss Harris around town.'

'No doubt,' Laurence agreed placidly. 'If he calls in here I take it that I may mention the latest developments?'

'Of course!' Tansy said brightly. 'Pa, do you mean to inform the authorities about Geoffrey's activities?'

'I see no reason for it,' her father said musingly. 'He hasn't committed any murders, or so he told you, and I'm inclined to believe him. Geoffrey never struck me as a violent man. He was — still is — what Finn would call a rather dubious character who supplemented his income with some discreet fencing of ancient treasures and got involved with the wrong people.'

'I doubt if Finn would put it quite so kindly,' Tansy said with a grin.

'His worst crime was deceiving you about his death,' Laurence said. 'If Geoffrey has any sense he will not return to England or within 500 miles of where I am residing.'

'That goes for me too, sir!'

Finn, entering in time to hear the closing remark, shook his head at them both as if he privately deplored their tolerance.

'What about the Vashti?' Tansy said, eager to close the subject.

'Back in the right hands — at least what the powers-that-be regard as the right hands,' Laurence said with satisfaction in his voice. 'No doubt various governments will be arguing for years as to which country actually owns the Vashti. Like the powers-that-be to hang on to whatever comes within their grasp! Fortunately we have no part in that. I kept your name out of it, Tansy. Merely said that I'd acted on information received and since I have a certain reputation for honesty and fair dealing they let it go at that!'

'And tomorrow is my last day at the museum,' Tansy said, rising. 'Finn, don't trouble to call a cab. I need the walk to the cab-stand.'

'Tansy, Geoffrey might be out of the picture,' Laurence warned, 'but that doesn't mean that your possible involvement in recent events has gone unremarked. I want you to take particular care. We still don't know the name of Geoffrey's ex-partner. If he knows that Geoffrey contacted you he might get curious.'

'I'll walk round by the road,' Tansy promised.

She meant to walk round by the road where several couples were strolling and enjoying the unseasonably balmy evening but at the gates of the park she changed her mind and walked in. There were a few late strollers, two or three young bloods in uniform with their girls on their arms, an elderly couple hurrying back presumably to the warmth of their fireside. Tansy slowed her step, testing her own feelings as she neared the lilac bush.

She had never visited the park in twelve years without feeling the sad emptiness of a lover lost. Tonight was different. She stood for a few moments by the bare-branched lilac bush and tried without success to conjure up the vanished scent of the faded blossom. She could not even catch the memory of the vanished perfume nor put herself back into her former loving, grieving self.

A step behind her made her start nervously but when she turned it was only Finn standing like some guarding deity on the grass verge.

'Can't jump back into the past, Miss Tansy,' he said.

'That's true,' she said soberly. 'And why are you following me?'

'Just to make sure you get safely into a cab,' he said firmly. 'I ain't forgotten that you have the habit of being followed by the wrong people for the wrong reasons.'

'Pa told you the whole story?'

'We don't know the whole story yet, Miss Tansy,' he reproved. 'Mr Geoffrey might've left the country and I'll be checking on that first thing tomorrow, and that partner what double-crossed him is probably still around and there's two men poisoned. Now you can argue with me that you're a grown woman but in my view since your pa can't follow you then that's my job when there's any mischief in the air. Not that you're my daughter, mind!'

'You never had . . . ?' She hesitated.

'Far as I know, miss, I won't be leaving my savings to any blood relations,' Finn said. 'The truth is that I never had much of a family to start off with and I don't have the kind of face that sends the ladies wild. Mind you, there was one time when I nearly had a sweetheart.'

'Honestly, Finn?'

Accepting his arm, she continued her walk.

'You've no call to sound so surprised, Miss Tansy,' he reproved. 'There's some women that appreciate a cultured mind more than a handsome face.'

'Yes, of course.'

'When I was a whippersnapper,' Finn was continuing solemnly, 'just getting into my line of work, so to speak — pickpocketing, mainly, though I already did a bit of fencing on the side — I was following a pretty girl, no more than nineteen, nicely dressed and with a purse fairly asking to be stolen the way it was sticking out of her side pocket. Well, my fingers were fairly itching and then she suddenly looked around and she had the sweetest face you could hope to see on any day! Fair took the wind out of my sails, so to speak, and she smiled at me real trusting like. Then she went on walking, not hurrying or trying to push her purse deeper in her pocket and I just stood there — a reformed man, Miss Tansy. A reformed man!'

'But I thought — ' Tansy began,

'Reformed from pickpocketing,' Finn explained kindly. 'I still went on the fencing and a house burglary now and then just to keep my hand in, so to speak.'

'You always got caught,' Tansy reminded him.

'That's true, miss, but when your pa pointed out to me that I was spending more time in gaol than in following my professional instincts I took him up on his offer and it turned out that I had quite a bent for cooking and suchlike.'

'Finn, you are the best chef I have ever known,' Tansy said warmly, 'and more importantly one of my best friends. I know that Pa values you highly.'

'As I do him, Miss Tansy,' Finn returned, 'and as for Mr Geoffrey, I think you should put him right out of your head for as much of the time as you can — same way I put the young lady with the sweet face out of my head. It might've turned out all right and then again it might not. With which thought I will walk on with you to the cab-stand and see you safely into a vehicle for there's still two men died unnatural and a statue that was stolen now in the hands of the right people and, so far, your dear name kept out of it.'

With which pronouncement he tucked her hand under his arm and bore her onward rather like a prize trophy.

But Frank was still squiring Susan Harris around, Tansy reflected gloomily.

Settled in the cab she decided that her most sensible course of action was to do nothing. Most sensible courses, however, ran contrary to her inclinations. Stepping out of the cab and paying the fare, she changed her mind about going into the house and instead walked on along the street, fully conscious of the fact that she was taking a risk — of what and from whom remained unclear but she had her small pistol in her pocket and her ears were sharp. In any case she had no intention of turning down the side alleys and heading for the river-bank.

As she walked, recent events struggled for supremacy in her mind. Two young men, both working in museums where Carl Royston had an interest, had died with all the symptoms of gastric fever, which had only been revealed as antimony poisoning after Susan Harris had received her belated note from Brook Wilton. It was unfortunate that

Frank seemed to have elected himself as Miss Harris's protector — Finn, she thought irritably, might have done the job just as well, and in any case Miss Harris didn't strike her as being in great need of protection!

She herself had discovered that the Geoffrey she had mourned for so long was still alive and very far from being the Geoffrey she had supposed him to be — but a murderer? No, he hadn't the ruthlessness necessary for that final deed. She resolved to dismiss him from her mind for good and was instantly pleasantly surprised by the relief that flooded her.

But who then had killed the two assistant curators? Who had been sufficiently alarmed by her own activities to follow her and thrust her into the river? Who had, on some Saturday when the Royston Museum was closed, brought the stolen figure of Queen Vashti in its case into the storeroom where, it was obvious, a place of concealment had been prepared?

Her thoughts were whirring around in circles. For a couple of insane moments she even bethought herself of the two landladies!

'Miss Clark!'

She spun round, relaxing as she recognized Robert Blake.

'What are you doing here?' she enquired.

'Not following me with a view to being my knight in shining armour should a dragon appear, I hope?'

'I'm afraid I'm Tilde's knight in armour and the only dragon I've met is Mrs Timothy,' he rejoined with unexpected humour.

'Not really so much of a dragon,' Tansy said lightly.

'Your suggesting the sausages worked a real treat,' he said warmly. 'You must be awfully good at reading people's characters and knowing what's what!'

'Not always,' Tansy said, suddenly sobered.

'That man who was following you — ' He hesitated slightly as they turned to walk back along the street.

'The one you thought you saw.'

'I saw him all right, Miss Clark.' He spoke suddenly with a simple dignity. 'I saw him though not clearly on account of his being in the shadows most of the time. Is there any chance he might come again?'

'No, Robert.' Feeling an immense relief sweep through her entire being, she answered him not only decisively but also almost gaily. 'No, that man will not be bothering any of us again.'

They had reached her front gate and she paused to hold out her hand.

'It's very kind of you to take such an interest in my safety but it's not necessary,' she told him.

'Actually I hoped I might get a glimpse of Tilde as she opened the door,' he confessed.

'On Saturday you will have her company and her undivided attention,' Tansy said severely. 'Go on home, Robert Blake, or you won't be fit for work in the morning.'

'Yes, Miss Clark. Good night, Miss Clark.'

He touched his forelock, sent her an embarrassed grin and hurried away but not, she noticed, until he had directed one long questing glance towards the kitchen window.

Had she ever really felt such a pure, undivided emotion, Tansy thought wistfully? Had she ever been so young?

It was no time to be speculating in the abstract. Two men were still dead; she herself had survived an attempt on her life; and the following day was the last time she would go in to work at the Royston Museum.

15

It was a morning to make one believe it was late summer again. Making her way to the museum, Tansy breathed in the cool dry air and briefly reverted to childhood as she scuffled her feet through a jumble of multicoloured leaves the roadsweeper hadn't yet reached.

Mr Benson was in his cubbyhole as usual, for all the world as if he expected hordes of visitors to arrive at any moment. Despite his dried-up appearance he had an optimistic nature, she reckoned, and greeted him with equal cheerfulness.

'So this is your last morning, Miss Clark?' He looked at her over the wire-rimmed spectacles he wore for reading. 'I shall be quite sorry to lose you though in the beginning I rather deemed the employment of another assistant somewhat superfluous to requirements. I expect that for your own part you will find your charity work more rewarding. What exactly do you do? One hears these days of well-educated young ladies venturing into the most unsavoury parts of the city and one fears for their safety.'

'I'm afraid that I don't do anything so dramatic,' Tansy said apologetically. 'I take a collecting box round on flag days and I help organize harvest festivals and bring-and-buy stalls for the poor — nothing very spectacular.'

'But still worthwhile.'

He favoured her with one of his rare smiles and then, recalling them both strictly to business, informed her that he had some new brochures to be sorted out.

In the expectation of hordes, Tansy thought with cynical amusement as she patiently put the carefully handwritten pamphlets in order and collected the others, though a swift perusal showed scarcely any difference between them. Mr Benson, she reflected with a twinge of pity, invented tasks for himself probably to prevent his brain from atrophying.

The figure of Carl Royston rose up in her mind — the piercing eyes and unexpectedly brisk walk. Carl Royston had founded a museum, filled it with mainly second-rate stuff and then had proceeded to neglect it for years. Why?

Joseph Fanshaw had worked here, had died in his lodgings. An unexceptional young man who must have found his job insufferably tedious . . . unless? Unless?

Stopping in her tracks near the figure of the Roman soldier, she was struck by such a beautifully simple notion that she couldn't believe she hadn't thought of it before.

'Yes, Miss Clark?'

William Benson, his earlier geniality extinguished, looked up from his desk with definite impatience.

'I thought of something,' Tansy said.

'Are your thoughts of such rare occurrence that you need to announce that one has arrived?' he enquired, his tone edged with faint sarcasm.

'Mr Royston founded this museum, filled it with respectable but not exceedingly exciting exhibits and then completely lost interest in it?'

'Regrettably, yes.'

'Who appointed the assistant curator?'

'Mr Royston did so. I thought it unnecessary but of course made no protest. In any case, I was not averse to some company from time to time. Forgive me but what is the point of all these queries?'

'I'm not an antiques expert,' Tansy plunged on, 'but I've always enjoyed looking at them and my — an acquaintance of mine — a former acquaintance — taught me a lot when we visited museums together. I have some feeling for the antique and the beautiful.'

'Very commendable!'

He had begun to look decidedly irritable.

'Carl Royston is a wealthy man and a man of taste,' Tansy said. 'Carl Royston wouldn't fill a museum he had just founded with second-rate stuff. He might not put the rarest objects in it but they would be authentic.'

'Yes, of course.'

'The fact that he never visits must be part of his unsociability. Would you agree?'

'Yes, that may well be true,' he said slowly.

'A philanthropist may found an orphanage but not trouble to visit the children there.'

'True,' he said again.

'Mr Benson, I believe some of these exhibits are fakes,' Tansy said.

'Miss Clark!'

'No, please hear me out! You can't dismiss me because I leave today anyway. I have no formal training but when I look at something or, better still, touch it, what is genuinely old has a certain resonance. My fingers tingle or, if it's behind glass, 'my eyes seem to see — It's like looking at real flowers instead of artificial ones. Antonio . . . '

'The Roman figure,' William Benson said with a faint sigh.

'That's a model no more than twenty or thirty years old, dressed in a centurion's traditional costume. It doesn't pretend to be anything more than a copy of someone of whom probably no physical trace remains — '

'Yes?'

At least she had his attention fully now.

'Three of the Portland vases are fakes,' Tansy said. 'The amber necklace from the Anglo-Saxon period — I believe the beads are of a much later date. The embroidered Chinese fan — that's a copy. I picked it up the other day and it felt . . . wrong. It didn't carry the weight of years. I am wondering if Joseph Fanshaw wasn't selling off the genuine exhibits on the rare occasions you were not here, and replacing them with fakes.'

'Miss Clark!' His face reflected his shock and distaste. 'May I remind you that Mr Fanshaw is dead. One ought never to slander the dead! He is not here to defend himself against such severe and unproven accusations! You must show some charity, Miss Clark. You speak of having a feeling for the genuine but it requires more than an emotional response to say definitely if a certain object is truly what has been claimed for it. You have had no formal training and cannot set yourself up as an expert.'

'I'm not,' Tansy said sharply.

'Indeed you are, Miss Clark, and poor Mr Fanshaw is not here to defend himself. I suggest we cut this conversation short and you return to your work for the brief period of employment left to you.'

His tone sounded not merely cool but positively icy.

On the spur of the moment Tansy said, 'Regarding what remains of my period of employment, I have decided to work for a few days more here next week. Perhaps you would be good enough to send a note to Mr Royston to inform him of my change of plans?'

For an instant she imagined he was going to refuse but he merely compressed his lips and gave a very audible sigh.

Tansy sent him her sweetest smile and went back to where Antonio, who in her opinion had more vitality than the curator, stood waiting in his glass cage.

'Waiting for what?' she queried aloud. 'I wager if you could talk you'd have some interesting things to tell me!'

After which the rest of the morning limped along, a couple wandering in hand in hand, not, it seemed, to admire the exhibits but to find a space where they could indulge in a private embrace.

The rest of the day crawled past with only one other visitor — an elderly lady who seemed under the impression that the objects on display were for sale.

'I had a note dispatched to Mr Royston,' William Benson informed Tansy when she emerged into the entrance hall in her outdoor garments. 'He sent an immediate reply, tacitly approving your decision. We will meet on Monday morning, Miss Clark, unless in the meantime you change your mind yet again.'

What she hoped to achieve in the extra days she had awarded herself she honestly didn't know but the certainty that valuable artefacts had been sold off and replaced by fakes and that Joseph Fanshaw had been responsible lingered in her mind. Had he double-crossed his associate as Geoffrey had been cheated by his partner? If so, there was a definite motive for his murder.

She was somewhat disappointed that evening when after a light supper, or rather Finn's version of one, she sat with him and her father and eagerly expounded her theory.

'If you are correct,' Laurence said, stressing his first word, 'then you obviously suspect Carl Royston of killing Joseph Fanshaw.'

'Carl Royston is a ruthless man. I'm certain of it!' she said.

'Then you haven't thought deeply enough about the matter,' he chided 'Let us assume, on no evidence, that Fanshaw was selling off and replacing the genuine exhibits. Why would Carl Royston go to the trouble of murdering him? Mr Royston takes no interest in the museum he founded and, even supposing that by other means he discovered the assistant curator to be a thief, all he had to do was inform the police and have him arrested. Carl Royston has, as far as I know, never broken any law. He would use the law, perfectly correctly, to dispose of a thief.'

'And what about the fellow at the other museum?' Finn put in. 'Had he been stealing and did Carl Royston murder him too?'

'I suppose not,' Tansy said reluctantly. 'But Carl Royston holds a directorship at the Kensington Museum.

'And never troubles to attend any of the meetings,' her father pointed out.

'I suppose you're right,' she said with a grimace.

'Mr Frank would agree if he was here,' Finn supplied.

But Frank hadn't been there, Tansy thought, taking her leave of them shortly afterwards and walking round by the road to the cab-stand. Frank Cartwright was still squiring little Miss Susan Harris of the dark ringlets and the pink garments round the city.

★   ★   ★

'Today,' Tilde announced brightly and unnecessarily at breakfast the next morning, 'is Saturday!'

'All day,' Tansy said somewhat gloomily, then recollecting, looked up with a swift apologetic smile. 'Robert Blake is taking you out this evening.'

'Just for a bite to eat and a bit of a walk,' Tilde said, her pretty face flushing.

'He's a very nice young man,' Tansy said warmly.

'Yes, Miss Tansy, he has very nice manners,' Tilde said. 'I was wondering if he might not have French blood.'

'French blood?' Tansy echoed in surprise.

'In the seventeenth century,' Tilde said earnestly, 'many French Huguenots fled from the religious wars in Paris and settled in England. It's possible that — '

'Anything is always possible,' Tansy said kindly.

It was clear that pointing out that the Blakes had been living in Chelsea for at least three centuries and were Londoners to the marrow would make no dent on Tilde's romantic imagination.

As far as Tansy herself was concerned, the weekend yawned ahead with no prospect of Frank arriving and her latest theory shot down in flames by her father and Finn.

Mrs Timothy, coming in to lay the freshly ironed newspaper on the table, gave her employer a concerned glance.

'Are we a mite seedy this morning?' she enquired.

'A mite bored,' Tansy said. 'It's come to something when I actually find myself looking forward to going into the museum on Monday.'

'Ah well! As we get older time levels out,' the housekeeper said philosophically.

'Does it indeed!'

'Not that I'm complaining!' the other hastened to assure her. 'I've had some fine times in the past and when my back's acting up I take out a memory or two and look at them. Now I've never actually been wedded as you know, Miss Tansy, but bedded a few times in my carefree youth — some more exciting than others, if you catch my meaning, and when there's a crick in my back — and though I never complain, I get a great many cricks — I remind myself that every bit of pleasure brings its pain later on. Sausages or fish for supper tonight?'

'Neither,' said Tansy, making up her mind on the instant. 'I'm going out for lunch and supper. You make whatever you fancy!'

At least, she reflected as she donned jacket and bonnet, if cricks in the spine depended

248

on one's past love life she could look forward to a pain-free old age!

There were cafés where unaccompanied ladies could lunch alone and a few restaurants where it was now possible to dine alone without too many eyebrows shooting skywards.

It wasn't until she was actually seated in the small café opposite the Royston Museum that she was forced to admit to herself that a few discreet questions to the waitress who knew her as a familiar figure by this time might yield some new information. Waitresses saw things that customers did not.

'You don't usually come in on a Saturday, miss,' the regular waitress said as she took Tansy's order. 'The museum's closed save for deliveries now and then, and not many of them.'

'Have you ever been in the museum?' Tansy enquired.

The girl shook her head.

'My work here takes up most of the week,' she said, 'and when I'm not here my fiancé and I like to walk in the parks when the weather's fine.'

'You're engaged?'

'Yes, but I don't wear my ring at work in case it gets lost or damaged,' the girl said. 'It's a beautiful ring with a real sapphire in it. We picked it out together. There were some very old rings there all cleaned and polished — the man in the shop said they were 400 years old — but who wants an old ring that lots of other people have worn?'

'Yes,' Tansy said absently as the waitress went off to fulfil her order.

Four-hundred-year-old rings didn't come on to the market every day, she thought. What was it her father sometimes said? 'Sometimes when you can't crack open a case a piece of gossip or something unconnected with anything falls straight into your lap and you see the way clearly.'

'The shop where you bought the ring together,' she said casually when the waitress returned with her soup and toast, 'where is it exactly? One of the Bond Street jewellers?'

'Oh no, miss. It's a shabby little shop down a side street,' the other said instantly. 'We saw it by chance with some pretty rings in the window but the old ring the man tried to sell us was in a case at the back of the shop and much too expensive. You did say oxtail soup?'

'I did. Thank you. I might buy some jewellery myself for a friend of mine,' Tansy said, a picture of Tilde coming into her mind.

'It's first turning on the left just past the big museum in Kensington,' the waitress told her and hurried in response to another customer's beckoning hand.

Was this the clue that would prove her theory, as yet nebulous, that Joseph Fanshaw had been selling off the genuine exhibits in the museum?

She finished her soup, added a handsome tip to her payment, and left the café, hailing a cab to the Kensington Museum.

The side street was easy enough to locate. Hesitating for a moment she turned into it and walked slowly over the rough cobbles.

The little shop looked dingy and dim, guaranteed not to attract customers.

Tansy took a deep breath and pushed open the door, setting a bell tinkling.

The inside was as dingy as the outside was gloomy and she paused for a moment to accustom her eyes to the faint lighting that came from a couple of gas lamps suspended from the ceiling.

There was a long counter that almost divided the interior into two equal halves and, below the counter, glass shelves protected by more glass which looked secure enough but was so dirty that it was almost impossible to make out what was on display.

'May I help you, madam?'

The man who emerged from the shadows at the back of the shop seemed to materialize like some ghost left to haunt the place after the previous owners had left.

'I wondered if you had any antique jewellery,' Tansy said collecting her wits. 'A friend of mine is having a birthday soon and I thought a brooch or a ring — she is very fond of old things. Pretty stones and such. I would be willing to pay a good price.'

'Now we do on occasion have antique pieces come into our hands,' the man said, sounding as if he headed a consortium of jewellers, though Tansy rather doubted it.

'Amber is a particular favourite of my friend's,' Tansy volunteered, her thoughts running along Anglo-Saxon lines.

'We have a rather pretty necklace in stock composed of chalcedony but I do believe the amber beads left us some days ago — let me just check to find out.'

He rummaged in the dim space behind the counter, produced a small book and began to turn the pages rapidly.

'Would this be what might please your friend?'

He had rummaged further and bobbed up with the amber necklace in his hand.

'May I?'

Tansy reached across the counter, took the necklace and ran it between her fingers. It looked exactly like the necklace on display in the Royston Museum but it felt centuries older. She had the distinct impression of a dozen or more hands caressing the smooth surface of the golden-brown beads strung on their silver chain.

'Does this have provenance?' she asked.

The other shook his head.

'Written provenance is often difficult to obtain,' he said apologetically. 'From time to time a keen amateur collector of my acquaintance — my very slight acquaintance — brings me in a piece that he thinks might appeal to the more discerning buyer. He has not been in for quite some time but his judgement is generally sound. The necklace is worth a great deal more than the price we fixed upon some time ago.'

'Which is?'

'Ten pounds,' the other said. 'Diamonds would fetch more but it's seldom — '

'Ten pounds!' Tansy said briskly. 'I'll take it.'

The other, she guessed, was a fence of stolen goods without fully realizing it or perhaps his lack of interest was a measure of his indifference as to how the amber beads had been found and originally sold to him.

'It is probably worth more,' he said now.

'You stipulated ten,' Tansy said.

'Yes. Indeed I did.'

He wrapped the beads in a piece of brown

paper, took the ten pounds she fished from her purse in somewhat unseemly haste and dived into the dim recesses of the shop again.

She was utterly convinced that it was the original necklace that had once adorned some Saxon lady, the tingling of her fingertips her only proof but when she went into the museum on Monday morning she would test it against the one now displayed there.

A second thought struck her. It was possible — not likely but possible — that Mr Royston himself, though she couldn't imagine for what reason, might have been denuding his museum of its genuine exhibits and if the odd little man who had sold her the amber was in the habit of making regular weekly reports to him then she herself might be in some danger.

What she ought to do was take a cab to her father's house and acquaint him with her latest theory. She looked about her for a vacant cab and stepped back hurriedly on to the pavement as one went past at a lickspittle speed, but not so fast that she didn't recognize the dark-haired girl in the pink garments and the elegant profile of her companion.

So Frank and Miss Susan Harris were having a Saturday afternoon jaunt together.

And I, Tansy decided grimly, am keeping my own investigations strictly to myself until I can astonish everybody with a neatly wrapped-up solution!

16

In the evening it rained, fine, cutting sheets of water that slanted across the garden and whipped the surface of the river into boiling foam. It would have been refreshing to take a brief walk along the bank in mackintosh cape and boots but Tansy, reminding herself that she was bent on a solution to the murders, decided to be sensible and stay indoors. The man in the shabby jewellery shop had seemed unsuspicious but if he was actively engaged in selling stolen goods purloined from the Royston Museum it was possible he might have recognized her and spoken of her visit to someone else.

Tilde, her best frock covered by a voluminous cloak that seemed to weigh down her slight figure, had departed at eight, Robert Blake in a stiffly starched shirt and dark suit, arriving with a large umbrella which he held as gallantly over Tilde as if the latter had been a member of the aristocracy to which she imagined her unknown father had belonged.

'One can only hope the lad's to be trusted,' Mrs Timothy sighed, bringing in Tansy's supper. 'He seems very respectable but there's a ravening animal inside every man waiting to leap out and devour!'

She ended on a sigh which led Tansy to suspect that on occasion Mrs Timothy had herself been devoured and had relished it. It was sobering to reflect that she herself was still untasted fruit.

Tansy had decided to take herself off to bed early in case Tilde imagined she was being checked on but Robert Blake had not, apparently, been in a ravening mood. Tilde floated in on a tide of remembered enjoyment, however.

'Oh, but it was lovely!' she said enthusiastically, appearing in the open door of the sitting room. 'The café had tiny little grilled fish and different kinds of bread and very elegant curd cake and various kinds of tea and coffee. Rob — Mr Blake has beautiful manners, always quick to notice if the sugar wasn't within reach.'

'And he kissed you good night?' Tansy enquired.

'He kissed my hand,' Tilde said. 'Just like his ancestors would have done!'

'Exactly so!' Tansy said gravely, and dismissed her maid to the kitchen where she could regale Mrs Timothy with an account of her two enchanted hours.

Sunday meant church though Mrs Timothy and Tilde generally attended evening service. There was still a fine mist over the river and the remaining leaves on trees and bushes were soaked and sodden when Tansy, having endured throughout her breakfast a reiteration of Robert Blake's surpassing intelligence and charm, took herself off to service.

Walking back to her house, she half expected to see Finn lurking in the distance, half hoped to bump into Frank, but nobody she knew hove in the area and she reached her house and the beef and carrots that Mrs Timothy had prepared without incident.

The afternoon and evening passed also without incident. Tansy sat down and began to write her own thoughts and theories on the current problem.

★ ★ ★

Why does Carl Royston never visit his museum?

Why are some of the exhibits fakes and others only of secondary importance?

Why should two men who seem not to have been acquainted have been killed in precisely the same manner within weeks of each other?

Carl Royston had a son. Where is he now?

Why did Vashti, Carl Royston's wife, leave him and their child?

Someone brought the statuette in its wooden case to the museum. Why would Carl Royston do that when he had a case ready prepared for Vashti in his house?

Why is Frank so interested in Susan Harris?

★   ★   ★

This last she scribbled out, feeling cross with herself for having thought of the question. Miss Harris of the pink garments had no part in any mystery save that she had known Brook Wilton and had received after his death and her return to work at the Kensington Museum a scrawled note telling her of his illness. Frank had obviously taken a fancy to the dark-haired beauty and one couldn't blame a man when someone else had kept him waiting too long.

Evening had drifted into a moonlit night, the air still tingling with unshed rain and a cool breeze rippling the river. Mrs Timothy and Tilde had taken themselves off to their respective beds, Tilde to dream of young men with French ancestors, Mrs Timothy to rest her aching back.

On impulse Tansy put on boots and cloak,

checked the pistol in her pocket and let herself out on to the terrace A brisk walk before bed struck her as sensible. She would walk at a good distance from the edge of the bank and turn back when she reached the little wooden bridge.

The river-bank was deserted. For no good reason she felt a tremor of nervousness as she stepped over the low wall of her garden and turned to the left. This, she told herself, was stupid. If she was going to flinch at every breeze-driven shadow she might as well go and live in the middle of the city and be done with it!

She deliberately slowed her pace, keeping clear of the damp grass and nearer to the back walls of the houses that abutted on to the riverside.

The little bridge gleamed wetly in the moonlight. Tansy stepped on to it and paused, turning to survey the way she had come, seeing only the trembling shapes of falling leaves and the more solid outlines of tree trunks and walls. The night then was quiet, bereft of walkers and of fishermen. She drew a breath of relief mingled with exasperation at her own foolishness and leaned against the rail.

An instant later, amid the splintering of wood, she was clinging desperately to one of the planks on which people crossed the bridge — a plank which should have been riveted closely with its fellows but now, having obviously been loosened, tilted sideways, tearing itself from its moorings.

Tansy held on with one hand while with the other she attempted to unfasten the ribbon that secured the heavy cloak about her neck, but the ribbon slipped between her fingers and she raised her voice as loudly as her laboured breathing could permit.

An instant later a running footstep paused at the edge of the bridge and a voice said calmly 'Take my hand, Miss Clark. No need to panic.'

Her wrist was being grasped and she struggled upwards, feeling her skirts brush wetly against the wooden uprights of the damaged bridge. An instant later she was seated on the damp grass, her garments feeling like lead weights, her hair escaping from its snood and her breathing slowly steadying.

'I had a thought as how something might be tried pretty soon,' Robert Blake said.

'What,' Tansy demanded, finding her normal voice, 'are you doing here?'

'Not sawing up bridges so folk can drown,' he returned coolly. 'I generally take a stroll this way in the early evening or sometimes later after supper — I used to hope for a glance of Tilde through the window of your house to speak truly and though she and I are friends now I still like to wander past, make sure all is well. Three ladies in a house with no male protection, not even a dog, ain't — isn't correct to my way of thinking.'

'Very gallant of you,' Tansy said, struggling to her feet. 'No, it really was gallant. But why should we need particular protection, for heaven's sake, or do you guard all the families in the neighbourhood?'

'No, there isn't time and there's only one Tilde,' he said simply. 'Miss Clark, I made bold months ago to enquire into Tilde's employer and fellow workmate, to coin a phrase, to make sure she was being treated right and not put upon. It sounds foolish for I'd done no more then than serve her in the shop but she's such a delicate young lady — '

'And?'

'My dad told me that your dad was a police inspector but now didn't actively participate in the solving of crimes,' Robert said. 'There was a rumour that you solved a couple of crimes yourself, acting on your dad's behalf, and Tilde is sure that you've got some reason for working at that old museum. So I've been keeping an eye open, so to speak. I hope you don't take it as an imposition?'

'I am twice indebted to you then,' Tansy said warmly.

'First someone pushes you into the river and that's after you've been followed so it made sense to keep an eye open when you decided to take a late-night stroll.'

'But the bridge must've been damaged earlier,' Tansy said, gathering her wits rapidly. 'Any person might've stepped on it.'

'True,' he considered, 'but the air's getting more wintry now and most people don't take lonesome walks near midnight excepting your good self, Miss Clark, and since it's clear you're investigating some foul deed then it's clear the villain is getting desperate. That's an old bridge anyway and some of the planks are already sagging. I've warned Tilde about you both being in some danger if you go wandering alone. T'ain't wise, Miss Clark!'

'You are perfectly correct, Mr Blake,' Tansy said tactfully. 'I shall certainly restrict my late-night walks until the present culprit, whoever they are, has been arrested.'

'It'll be a weight off my mind and Tilde's too,' he said gravely.

'Thank you again, and now I will say good night.'

'I'll walk back with you,' he said firmly. 'Anyway, I've a question to ask.'

'Yes?' Tansy paused briefly to wring the

hem of her garments where the water had splashed up. Her boots squelched unpleasantly on the damp ground.

'The truth is,' Robert Blake said in a rush, 'I'm wondering if I have a chance.'

'A chance of what?' Tansy enquired.

'With Tilde,' he said. 'I know it's early days and we've only just started walking out, so to speak, but I never in my life met any girl like her. It's just that . . . I'm bowled over, Miss Clark, fairly bowled over like lightning hit me. I'd give a good deal to know — with Tilde having no family except your good self and Mrs Timothy, and Mrs Timothy scares the daylights out of me! Well, she — Tilde, I mean — might have been drawn to confide in the older generation.'

Oh dear! Tansy thought, hardly knowing whether to be amused or offended, he meant me. She decided to be amused, suppressed a smile and said, 'Would you, by any remote chance, have a French ancestor in your family tree?'

'My grandparents lived over near Smithfield,' Robert said, sounding slightly downcast. 'They did visit France though on a couple of occasions. Grandpa was interested in how pigs were cured over in Brittany and Grandma went with him.'

'I think that might be sufficient to tip the

scales,' Tansy assured him. 'At least it's a French association. Yes, I think Tilde might be swayed if you just casually dropped into the conversation that your great-grandparents had a French connection.'

'It wasn't a very long one,' Robert said. 'The Revolution broke out and they had to sail home in a hurry.'

'Better yet!' Tansy enthused. 'Fugitives from the guillotine! But don't try to rush her into anything, will you?'

'That I won't,' he promised, 'but I've a strong feeling she has the same thoughts about me as I have about her and it'd be a pity to waste all our youth in wishing.'

'Yes,' Tansy said, suddenly sobered. 'Yes, you live life at the pace that suits you, Robert.'

'And you won't go walking along the river-bank again after dark until this villain, whoever he may be, is caught?'

'I promise you,' Tansy said soberly. 'However, whoever damaged the bridge so badly cannot have known that I'd be the one to step on it.'

'They might if they've been following you close, Miss Clark,' Robert said.

And Geoffrey had followed her not sure whether to announce his return or not. But she had been assured that Geoffrey had left the country for good. Who then still walked in the shadows?

They had reached the garden wall. Stepping over it, feeling the wet weight of her skirts against her legs, Tansy said, 'It would be as well not to mention this episode to Tilde. She is of a nervous disposition.'

'Like a flower,' he agreed promptly. 'No, I'll say nothing, Miss Clark.'

'Miss Tansy will suffice. Good night, Robert, and thank you again.'

Wondering what 'nervous' flower the lad had had in his mind, Tansy hurried up the garden and let herself in through the French windows. She was able to get into her dressing gown and put her splashed garments in the wash with the rest of the week's washing quietly where, she hoped, their damp condition wouldn't be noticed.

In the morning she felt, if not at ease in her mind, at least determined. This week she would seek and find answers, she decided firmly, her heart sinking slightly as she contemplated the long hours ahead with the occasional visitor wandering through the rooms and herself with either mop and duster or another of the ubiquitous brochures to be copied out!

As usual William Benson was in his cubbyhole sorting through a sheaf of papers, his smile slightly frosty as he raised his head.

'Good morning, Miss Clark. You haven't changed your mind yet again, have you? You will be here over the next few days? Mr Royston is not a man who appreciates shilly-shallying.'

'I will be here,' she returned, seizing cleaning materials before he could thrust any brochure at her and escaping to the small room at the back where she could take off her outdoor garments and prepare for the morning, which did however produce half a dozen visitors who asked a number of quite sensible questions.

Rather to her surprise, Frank was in the café when she went across to get her luncheon snack.

She spotted his fair head bent over a newspaper and felt a decided thrill of pleasure. At this moment she realized how much she had missed his company in recent days.

'Tansy!' Becoming aware of her presence he turned and rose, taking her hand in the old friendly manner. 'I called on your father last night and he said you had resolved to work at the museum for a further few days. You don't expect to discover anything fresh, surely?'

'If I didn't I wouldn't be there,' Tansy

retorted crisply. 'Someone has been bringing in illicit artefacts and I have a shrewd suspicion it's Carl Royston. He must have others working for him — '

'Fences? That's fairly customary once one starts dabbling in stolen antiques. What will you have?'

'Tea and scrambled eggs, please. Frank, about Geoffrey — '

'I watched him board the ship and I stayed until it had sailed out of the harbour,' Frank broke in. 'You're not thinking of following him, surely?'

'No, of course not,' Tansy said flatly.

'It must have been a dreadful shock to find out he was involved in smuggling antiquities,' Frank said in a tone carefully devoid of too much sympathy. 'Disillusionment can be painful.'

'Not as painful as I thought when I first heard from Geoffrey how he really spent his time when he was abroad. Shall we talk about the weather now? I have no other news save that Tilde and Robert Blake are getting along so well together that I rather fear I shall have to advertise for a new maidservant soon.'

'Pleasant to witness the stirrings of young love,' he said solemnly.

They glanced at each other and laughed.

Tansy, cutting up her toast, felt suddenly alive and hopeful.

'Which reminds me,' he continued, 'that I promised to go over to the Kensington Museum this afternoon. Miss Harris has just received a promotion and there will be a modest celebration to which I am invited.'

'By all means. Don't let me detain you,' Tansy said smilingly.

The toast was scorched along the edge and not enough salt had been put in the eggs. She drank her tea and rose, carefully counting out her money, tipped the waitress and gave Frank a slightly stiff nod.

'Enjoy the celebration,' she said brightly. 'I hope to go round and see Pa this evening if I've managed to find out anything.'

'Nice seeing you, Tansy.'

He rose politely, touched her lightly on the shoulder, and was eating his meal again when she turned to look at him from the door.

★　★　★

'You are four minutes late, Miss Clark,' Mr Benson said. 'Service in the café is usually swift but perhaps it was rather crowded today.'

'Somewhat,' Tansy said shortly.

There were a few more visitors during the afternoon which relieved the tedium, though she found herself glancing at her fob watch from time to time — as if, she thought ironically, something wonderful was going to happen for her.

'We have had quite a good day,' William Benson remarked when the last of the visitors had gone and she was sweeping up the few specks of dust he would be sure to grumble about if she didn't.

'Yes. The cooler, damper weather probably encourages people to come inside.' She paused in her sweeping, wondering what had brought him out of his cubby hole.

'Miss Clark, are you still of the opinion that genuine artefacts have been exchanged for fakes and smuggled out to be sold elsewhere?' he asked abruptly.

'Yes, Mr Benson, I'm afraid that I'm still of that opinion,' she said gravely. 'I have been turning it over in my mind and it occurred to me that Joseph Fanshaw may have tried to doublecross his partner — rogue against rogue, if you like.'

'Joseph Fanshaw,' he said tiredly, 'was a completely innocent young man. Innocent, Miss Clark!'

'Then who — ' Tansy stopped short.

'Joseph Fanshaw wasn't the most efficient

of assistants,' he said, 'but he was scrupu-lously honest in every respect. I am the one who has been selling off some of the artefacts now and then.'

'You?' Tansy stared at him. 'Mr Benson, why? Why would you? For money?'

'And money I have made has gone directly to charity,' he said.

'Then I don't understand,' Tansy said blankly.

In a moment she would wake up when Tilde tapped on the door!

'You had best sit down, Miss Clark.' He indicated a chair. 'The truth is that by and large I am a very mild man. There are few people I have disliked and only one I have ever really hated.'

'Who?' Asking the question, the answer flashed into her mind even before he spoke.

'Carl Royston,' William Benson said. 'His name — the mere thought of him — leaves me rigid with anger. Deadly deep-seated anger, Miss Clark.'

'But why?' she heard herself ask.

'I was married once, Miss Clark.' He leaned against the wall and looked across the small space between them. 'I was a young man once and my wife was the sweetest of wives. She died young, leaving me with a small son to rear. He wasn't a brilliant boy but he was intelligent and willing to work hard. I used to write and lecture on antiques but the payments were small and I had no original research to offer. I needed a regular occupation which would enable me to take care of my son — oh, he was a young man then and perhaps I overprotected him a little but he was the last living reminder of my darling wife. That was when Carl Royston contacted me. He had heard of my plight — made enquiries after attending one of my little lectures, I believe — and when a very rich man wants to hear about someone they are always able to achieve their aims. Money talks loudly in certain quarters, Miss Clark!'

'And?'

'Carl Royston contacted me. He had just founded this museum and he wanted a regular curator. The stipend was fair but not generous and the post was for life. He also offered my son, Frederick, regular employment in his own household. It was a seemingly generous offer. No man in my position would've turned it down, and Frederick was eager to make a success of his job.'

'As a footman?' she hazarded

'Precisely so!' He nodded his grey head emphatically. 'As a footman, with the opportunity of working his way up to head footman, with a uniform and a room in that mansion that Mr Carl Royston calls home. We were both grateful, Miss Clark. And then some coins were stolen.'

'Your son sold the coins,' Tansy breathed. A wave of pity broke over her.

'Carl Royston also had a son,' William Benson said. 'Benjamin Royston.'

'And he . . . ?'

'Pray allow me to continue,' he said coldly.

Tansy inclined her head uneasily.

'The Roystons had a son. Mrs Royston, whom I never met, left her husband and child within five years of the marriage and returned to her people in the Middle East. Benjamin Royston hardly knew his mother, for which one might spare a modicum of sympathy, but the fact is that he was bad from the beginning. Mr Royston seemed to think it was just boyish high spirits. I only saw him once. He was a young man by then and he struck me as a most unpleasant character. His father had spoiled him I daresay. There is always a great temptation for a lone parent to do that. Anyway, my lad was taken on as footman and I was appointed as curator here. At first all went well. My job here was to my liking and though I was somewhat surprised that Mr Royston took no further interest, I judged him to be a busy man.'

'And then some coins were stolen from his house,' Tansy breathed.

'Benjamin Royston stole them,' William Benson said. 'He had everything in the world he could possibly want but it amused him, I daresay, to cheat his father. Carl Royston called in the police before he realized who the thief was. He bribed my son to take the blame for the theft and Frederick went to prison for three years. He hanged himself in his cell six months into his sentence and he left a note for me telling me the true story.'

'Did the police — '

'Arrest young Royston? No, they were never told. The guard on duty the night Frederick took his own life handed me the letter privately. I never told anyone that I knew the truth. I wanted to get revenge in my own time, in my own way.'

'Revenge wouldn't bring your son back,' Tansy murmured, torn between horror and pity.

'Men like Carl Royston buy and sell at their own will,' he said. 'He wanted a knighthood which is partly why he founded the museum here and amused himself by stocking it with artefacts which, though interesting in themselves, were none of them rare or of outstanding value. As you have seen, very few people visit and Carl Royston didn't get his knighthood.'

'And you began selling off some of the things,' Tansy said.

'Any money I have made has gone straight to charity, Miss Clark. One does not seek to profit by revenge.'

'But Carl Royston doesn't know!'

'The joy, though that's not the right word, lies in my knowing that I have the better of him and since he is ignorant of the fact there is nothing he can do.'

Staring at him, Tansy had the sudden unnerving thought that he was a trifle mad. No doubt years of brooding over the miscarriage of justice and the suicide of his son had resulted in his brain sliding away from the normal.

She had risen from her chair, encouraged by a draught from the door that caused him to glance aside for an instant. Before he had seen her rise, she was edging round the glass case in which Antonio stood.

'Stay where you are, Miss Clark! My tale's not finished yet!' he said sharply, his attention drawn by the swinging of her skirt.

'I think Mr Royston, whatever his own wrongdoing, ought to know that he is being cheated!' she said angrily.

'No, Miss Clark!' He turned and lunged in the direction she was going.

Tansy, unwonted panic surging through her, turned back and, her foot slipping on the parquet, crashed into the case which, obviously insecurely fastened, tilted slightly and sent the silent figure within tottering grotesquely from his stand. The stand tilted, the figure fell, the head detaching itself from the hollow body and rolling across the floor where it lay.

'Oh, Good Lord!' Tansy exclaimed, wanting to laugh as the ugly little scene turned into farce.

'Miss Clark, this is beyond all — '

William Benson halted abruptly, staring at the plaster head. From its neck, caught suddenly as a long ray of unseasonable sunshine arrowed through one of the windows, protruded a yellowish brown bone.

For an instant only, time hovered, and then both were wrenching aside the hanging glass door of the case and were on their knees, Tansy with her hands clasped across her mouth, Mr Benson reaching into the hollow space and bringing out the thin, partly charred bones that culminated in part of an undoubtedly human skull.

'Carl Royston's wife left him within five years of the marriage,' Tansy said chokingly. 'When did the figure — '

'Mr Royston brought the figure to the

museum himself. It had head and limbs screwed into place and was fully clad,' he said, staring at the bone in his hand. 'It was about six months after the rumour that his wife had returned to the Middle East began to surface.'

'And nobody checked,' Tansy said, sitting back on her heels and feeling suddenly sick.

'I cannot understand why he would hide the bones here,' Mr Benson said, setting the relic down gently and bringing out a large handkerchief to wipe his brow.

'Because if someone had troubled to try to contact her and her disappearance became a subject of enquiry, his house and grounds would certainly be searched,' Tansy said. 'I doubt if anyone would've thought of looking here, where he never came. Mr Benson, I knew there was something about Antonio that fixed my attention. I knew there was!'

17

'We don't know,' he pointed out doubtfully, 'that these are the bones of Vashti Royston.'

'To whom else could they possibly belong?' Tansy said energetically. 'The figure is a modern one.'

'Made to Mr Royston's specifications,' Mr Benson agreed gloomily.

'And set up in a glass case in the style of garments worn by a Roman centurion. And if Carl Royston can murder his wife, the mother of his child, then he can certainly dispose of two young men who might possibly have started asking questions independently of each other or have seen something suspicious!'

'We cannot go making accusations without proof,' he objected, beginning to pack the pathetic remains back into the hollow figure. 'The most we can do is report this matter to the police and leave them to deal with it.'

'Mr Benson, do you really need me here for the rest of the afternoon?' Tansy demanded.

'What have you in mind? Miss Clark, you can hardly go off on a train of investigation of your own!' he objected.

'If you can wait here, I can return shortly before or shortly after closing time.'

'You intend to consult with your father? Very well. I am reluctant to grant you leave to go off during your specified hours of employment but if you insist — '

'I do insist,' Tansy said firmly.

'Help me set this figure upright and the case — at least the glass is not smashed!'

'Yes, of course!'

Relieved that she hadn't been forced to indulge in a long argument, she helped him set the figure upright and lever the case into position. It was, she decided, certainly her imagination but Antonio looked distinctly self-satisfied.

Going out of the museum, hailing a cab, she had already decided that Carl Royston was a man she would tackle alone without help from her father, Frank or Finn.

'If I cannot be a woman desired,' she thought grimly, 'I can at least be a woman respected for her fine detective work!'

Yet she felt a momentary shrinking as she paid the cabbie and made her way across the forecourt to the steps leading up to the main door.

'Mr Royston must not be disturbed during his afternoon siesta, miss,' the footman reproached as he admitted her into the echoing hall.

'This is a matter of some urgency,' Tansy said primly. 'Museum business.'

'Wait here, please.'

He directed her to the solitary chair and went, soft-footed, away. Within five minutes he had returned, his expression as stolid as ever.

'Mr Royston will see you in the small sitting-room, Miss Clark. Please come this way.'

She found herself being conducted with suitable gravity to the room at the back of the hall where Mr Royston occupied the same chair, hands clasped about the head of his walking stick. His eyes, hooded and keen, probed her face.

'Will you take some refreshment?' he enquired. 'Coffee? A glass of negus?'

'Nothing, thank you,' she said stiffly.

When one was about to question a man as to whether he had murdered his wife, it seemed rather gross to accept his hospitality.

He nodded brusquely to the footman, who withdrew, and turned his attention back to Tansy.

'I trust you are not come to tell me again that you wish to vary your terms of employment?' he said.

'I came to talk about Vashti,' she said.

'Ah yes! It appears the statue has been discovered and handed over to the authorities.' He gave a brief sigh. 'Your father is a law-abiding man which doesn't always work in a man's favour. I would have paid him most generously had he entrusted it to me. Now, unless it appears on the open market again, the beautiful cabinet I had made for it was made to no purpose.'

'I mean Vashti, your wife,' Tansy said.

'A lady you have never met and with whom you can have nothing whatsoever to do.'

'You don't visit the museum you founded,' she said.

'I do not.'

'But you arranged for the figure of a man dressed as a Roman centurion to be made and then exhibited in a glass case in the museum?'

'I did. What of it? I never instructed anyone to pretend the figure was anything more than a reproduction.'

'There are bones — human bones — inside the head and probably other bones in the figure itself,' Tansy said.

She thought his face went a little greyer and he drew in his breath but otherwise he remained motionless, staring at her.

'There was a slight accident,' she went on,

stealing herself against his basilisk gaze. 'Mr Benson helped me to right the figure but the head had come loose. Human bones, Mr Royston. Small, slender bones. The authorities are being informed.'

'I doubt that somehow,' he said drily, 'or the police would be ringing the doorbell. And if you had already informed your estimable father I doubt if he would have permitted you to come here alone — or is the house surrounded?'

'The bones looked as if they had been partly burnt,' Tansy said. 'Mr Royston, your wife never went back to her own people, did she? You — '

'She was the most beautiful creature any man could imagine,' he broke in. 'She made other women look clumsy and tawdry. Within a year of our marriage she had borne me a son, an heir to the millions I was already adding to my original inheritance. Benjamin. My boy, Benjamin. He was four years old, Miss Clark, with the face of angel and the soul of a devil. There are some people who are like that — born evil to bring heartbreak. From the moment he could toddle he was busy hurting and destroying. He liked to pull the heads off small birds, the wings off flies. Even tiny children have a sense of sin but my boy had none. He was deformed as surely as if he had some physical impairment. One day I sent him upstairs to his room because he had been tormenting the kitchen cat until the poor creature howled in pain. I sent him up to his room and said I would talk with him later.'

'And?' Unwillingly, she felt herself gripped by the narrative.

'My wife, Vashti, was sleeping. I never could bear to speak sharply to him but Vashti sometimes slapped him or scolded him. He went into her room and smashed her head in with a poker.'

'Surely — '

'He was tall and strong for his years and the first blow fractured her skull. He went on hitting her, Miss Clark. When I went up later to waken her from her nap I found him there, with the most angelic look on his face as he contemplated his handiwork. It was a summer afternoon and several of the servants had been given the day off; others were in the kitchen quarters or the stables. I like my family life to remain as private as possible. I took Benjamin to his room and locked the door and then I worked fast and ferociously to do what was necessary. I could not risk anyone seeing her as she was. I did what was necessary, Miss Clark.'

Tansy sat staring at him, horrified by the

revelations and yet certain that he was telling the truth.

'I saddled up my horse and rode it to Kensington Gardens and then, the swathed bundle in my arms — she was always tiny and very slender — I buried her. It was a temporary measure while I had time to think, to plan. For a couple of months the bushes covered her but before winter came I took up what remained and burned what I could. I am a man whose comings and goings my staff are trained not to question. I built a Guy Fawkes bonfire on the edge of a paddock where I kept a couple of ponies and I burned — but a few I could not bear to burn and I snatched them out. By then I had made it known that my wife had decided to return to her own people. I said that I lived in monthly expectation of her returning so no alarm was raised, no search mounted.'

'And your son?' Tansy whispered.

'He had forgotten all about the event within hours. He never mentioned her again. I sent him away to an excellent school when he was seven but I was asked to remove him. He had bullied some of the other boys. It was the same at every school, every college. Oh, he was bright and very intelligent and he had great charm. I flattered myself that he cared a little for me. Of course, he thought only of his inheritance. Then the coins were stolen. We had had months of peace and good comradeship and I was beginning to hope that whatever malady had affected him in his early youth was gone. I was mistaken. The tendency to violence was departed but in its place came the most flagrant dishonesty and I had called in the police before that fact dawned upon me. Poor young Frederick Benson was accused and sentenced for the crime and did away with himself in prison. He had guessed who the culprit really was. At least, I assume that was what occurred.'

'And now — where is Benjamin now?'

'Abroad. I sent him abroad with a generous allowance on the understanding he would never return, never try to contact me. I have no idea whether he is alive or dead.'

'And the bones of your wife remained in the museum. How could you?'

'Bones are bones, Miss Clark! Nothing more!' For a moment his mouth twisted into a grimace. 'Yet I tell you frankly that I could not bear to set foot in the museum I had founded. And yet it troubled me foolishly that I had no grave for Vashti where I could sit quietly and think of her beauty and her charm. Then I heard of a statuette of the original Queen Vashti, found in a tomb in the Middle East, and already being smuggled from hand to hand. I resolved to have that statuette and to enclose it in a cabinet of the finest sandalwood. Not long since, a man who had occasionally reported certain finds and obtained them for me — you will have known him as Geoffrey but I understand that from time to time he took different names — reported that his partner had discovered the whereabouts of the Vashti. He also named his price for bringing her to me — it was excessive! I contacted his partner and the statuette was delivered to the museum where a temporary hiding place was found for it. I paid him a reasonable amount — he was a person of small importance.'

'Was?' Tansy queried.

'I heard quite recently he had an unfortunate accident on board ship during his return voyage. No, it was a genuine accident. Geoffrey had sailed on a later vessel and in any case he never would have had the stomach for decisive action. You lost little when you believed him dead!'

'I found the statuette,' Tansy said.

'And took it straight to your father like a dutiful daughter. You are a young woman of spirit, my dear. My darling wife would have enjoyed your friendship.'

'Mr Royston, two other men have died — ' Tansy began.

'A couple of assistant curators! I assure you that when I employ a person I do not choose men or women of any importance. I never met either of them and I doubt if either of them ever heard about the Vashti — their deaths are of no importance.'

In that moment Tansy knew with a chilling of her heart where Carl Royston's son had inherited his violent tendencies, his ability to forget his own wrongdoing, his lack of normal human compassion. She felt slightly sick.

'All deaths are of importance,' she said with difficulty.

'Possibly the death of one who is loved,' he temporized.

'How could anyone deny someone they loved the dignity of a final resting place?' Tansy burst out, her face crimsoning with temper. 'You wanted to possess a beautiful wife you could gloat about, Mr Royston. You wanted — '

'Don't presume to tell me what I wanted,' he broke in sharply. 'Yes, I kept her largely within this house, which has every comfort. The garden at the back you have not seen but it contains rare plants, flowers of surpassing beauty. Vashti had grown up in a society where families go veiled. She regarded her life here with me as freedom enough! What my son did was horrific but it was never my fault.

He was born bad though it was a very long time until I admitted as much to myself. After the affair of the stolen coins and the suicide of the footman, I sent my lad to the Colonies. I told him to remain there, never to set foot in England again! I have neither written to him nor seen him since, though now and then a letter did arrive in the beginning, expressing no remorse or sorrow — he wiped that terrible deed from his mind on the day he committed the crime. In any case, how many people would have credited a child of four with such a black heart? Had I reported Vashti's death I would have been the first suspect. As it is, I did what was necessary to protect my son and my own reputation, and naturally when I heard of the Vashti statuette my first resolve was to acquire it through various traders with whom I occasionally do business.'

'And there's no proof of any of this,' Tansy said scathingly.

'There are the bones,' he said. 'I take it they are still inside the Roman figure?'

She nodded.

'I believe it is illegal to dispose of a body,' he said indifferently. 'However, it is also possible — not likely but possible — that Benjamin has made good out in the Colonies. Should I be questioned, I would be forced to admit that I acted to protect my son.'

'They don't hang children of four!' Tansy said.

'But even supposing my story was believed — and I swear to you that it's true — Benjamin would be brought back and interrogated. Might that not disturb the balance of his mind again? He might be married by now and have children of his own! I do advise you to think through the problem logically before you reach any conclusion. Good day to you, Miss Clark.'

He had tugged sharply at the bell rope by his chair and a tap at the door announced the footman, face expressionless as usual.

Rising, going out without any farewell or even a backward glance, Tansy felt cold with rage and disgust that such men as Carl Royston could exist and flourish. She would certainly speak to her father later but she feared that he too might see the difficulty of bringing a man like Carl Royston to the justice she felt strongly he deserved. For his son she could feel only a bewildered pity. If wickedness really could be inherited from a parent then in some ways Benjamin Royston had been innocent too, though his later record at school suggested otherwise. Certainly his father had done nothing to check his evil tendencies and had washed his hands of him after the business of the stolen coins and sent him away to the Colonies, where she doubted very greatly if he would have matured into a pillar of society.

Stepping out of the cab she had hailed and been driven in with her mind full of the hard-faced and flint-hearted millionaire, a possible solution to the deaths of the two assistant curators presented itself to her. Suppose that Joseph Fanshaw had also found the bones hidden in the hollow figure of the Roman and been foolish enough to go to Royston House and make known his discovery? Suppose he had in fact known Brook Wilton rather better than had been known and had confided in him too? And suppose instead of informing either William Benson or the police they had put their heads together and decided to do a little blackmail? Assistant curators were not handsomely paid, as she had realized herself. New speculations began to open up in her mind.

'Miss Clark, the museum closed officially ten minutes ago,' William Benson said, unlocking the front door. 'I saw you from the window strolling as if you had all the time in the world! Young people these days are sadly neglectful of their duties!'

'I do apologize, Mr Benson,' she said, relishing the implied compliment. 'I went to see Mr Royston, and he . . . he was absolutely frank with me as if he had no conscience at all!'

'You haven't informed your father? Surely it was rash to go alone to see Mr Royston? He is a ruthless man who will stop at nothing.'

'But I do think he told me the truth,' she said.

'The truth being?'

'May we sit down somewhere?' she begged. 'My thoughts are in a complete jumble.'

'You had best come into my office,' he said, dignifying his cubbyhole beyond its deserts. 'I shall break the rules for once and make a pot of tea. Usually I extinguish my small fire when I lock up but this is an unusual day. Please sit down.'

'Thank you.'

Taking a seat, watching the curator as he stirred up the fire and put the kettle on the hob, she felt, for the first time, a feeling of comradeship. He had suffered cruelly from the loss of his own wife and the tragic end of his own son and yet he had retained his dignity.

'I had some biscuits,' Mr Benson said, looking about him vaguely.

'Never mind the biscuits,' she said impatiently. 'Leave the tea to brew and sit down, Mr Benson, I don't suppose you were aware that some stolen artefacts were brought in here to the museum on Saturdays, when you were generally not on duty, and sold on again. Not all Mr Royston's wealth was inherited or obtained through honest means.'

'I sometimes wondered,' he confessed. 'However, the post suited me and I hardly ever went up to the storeroom. The truth is, Miss Clark, that after my poor son's suicide I hadn't the heart to begin my life anew. I stayed where you see me now and cultivated if not contentment, at least resignation.'

'And from time to time,' she reminded him, 'you sold off a genuine antique yourself and had it replaced by a copy.'

'For charity and I have always kept a careful accounting,' he said stiffly.

'And the assistant curators who died? Mr Benson, if you know anything more than you've yet told me I do beg you to speak now,' Tansy urged, 'otherwise Mr Royston — '

'Mr Royston employed them both privately to search for the Vashti statuette,' Mr Benson said. 'Word of its existence had circulated freely and when an assistant curator was thrust upon me then I began to fit supposition to guesswork and arrive at the truth.'

'It was Joseph Fanshaw who discovered the

whereabouts of the Vashti?'

'I believe so, yes. That young man couldn't avoid dropping certain hints that he knew something about a certain figure in which Mr Royston was interested.'

'And Mr Royston could've killed him because he demanded too high a price for his silence!'

The other put up his hand hastily, shock in his face.

'My dear Miss Clark! You cannot start accusing people of murder on the basis of no evidence! The bones we found may not have anything to do with Carl Royston or his wife! As your father's daughter you must know that witnesses, sworn statements — all and more are necessary!'

'The bones are those of Vashti Royston,' Tansy said steadily. 'Her death was . . . one might call it a terrible accident. Mr Royston had grounds for keeping it secret and so disposed of the remains. That he could do so in such a cold-blooded fashion marks him as a man who desires to possess and has little notion of how to love, but you are right. He has killed nobody . . . '

She hesitated as she ended her sentence.

'What is it?' William Benson asked.

'I may be wrong, Mr Benson,' she said slowly, 'but it's possible that Joseph Fanshaw

— Might he not have found out what happened and been killed to prevent his talking? Mr Royston might have employed someone else . . . ?'

'I do assure you that if Mr Fanshaw had by some mischance overturned the figure of the Roman and discovered the remains of that poor woman then I would have heard about it,' he said stiffly.

'But you are not here on a Saturday when many goods — '

'Artefacts, Miss Clark, if you please! No, that's true though very occasionally I was invited to attend. The objects delivered were seldom of much interest and Mr Royston himself very rarely troubled to put in an appearance.'

'I still think that Joseph Fanshaw either found the bones or discovered stolen artefacts were being passed through this museum. He might've known Brook Wilton and told him and the two of them threatened to expose Carl Royston — '

'My dear young lady, you have missed your vocation and should be writing novels!' he broke in. 'It is perfectly possible the young men were killed — if they were killed at all! — for some reason that had nothing to do with stolen artefacts or those pathetic bones! Both were employed on very little experience as assistant curators with the added task of passing on what they might learn about the Vashti statuette to Carl Royston, it appears. People are not murdered because they fail to learn a few facts!'

'I suppose not,' she said unwillingly. 'But Carl Royston still disposed of his wife's body unlawfully.'

'Yes, indeed, it seems so,' he said, frowning into his tea. 'But what purpose would be served in exposing him now? He could simply deny everything and there is no proof. It would be most interesting to learn exactly how the poor woman died. However — Miss Clark, it is well past closing time and we are wasting the early evening. You will doubtless acquaint your father with news of your discoveries! I believe he will agree with my assessment that the whole affair is best dropped now.'

'It is something to think about,' she admitted reluctantly.

But the fact remained that a crime had been committed even though the murderer had been a child, had been covered up, that a body had been treated with something much less than reverence and the killer allowed to go free though there was no guarantee that someone with a diseased and twisted mind would not kill again. And Carl Royston had been concerned with the finding and concealing of the stolen Vashti statue. A man who used his wealth to enrich his own cupidity, she thought gloomily, paying William Benson a subdued good afternoon before stepping out into the street.

She walked home in an uneasy mood, various possibilities revolving in her mind, none of them very feasible. Mrs Timothy, meeting her at the door, looked slightly flustered.

'Is it your back?' Tansy asked automatically.

'No indeed, Miss Tansy! My back has not been playing up as much as usual,' the housekeeper said brightly. 'No, the fact is that Tilde went round to order the meat and hasn't returned yet. I know her young man is in the shop this afternoon and I am just hoping that the time is not drawing near when an innocent dove is soiled due to my careless good humour.'

'The young man is the soul of honour,' Tansy said solemnly. 'I believe that Robert Blake will prove a godsend in the future.'

'She needs someone to steady her — all that French blood,' Mrs Timothy said.

'Yes indeed, Mrs Timothy,' Tansy said and went past her up the stairs.

What she ought to do was change, go over to her father's house, and lay all in his lap. But Mr Benson had very likely been right when he had made it plain that in his opinion Carl Royston had the money to wriggle free from even a serious charge.

'He wouldn't find it so easy if Pa was still on the force,' she muttered, pulling off her clothes and deciding on a long soothing bath.

When she came downstairs again, Tilde had returned, her pretty face flushed and happy.

'Robert asked me what I would like as a birthday present,' she said eagerly. 'I told him that a spray of flowers would be acceptable. A lady doesn't accept anything except flowers or perfume or a pair of gloves from a gentleman. My mother was always very particular about that.'

Tansy, quickly squashing the thought that Tilde's mother had almost certainly been in the habit of accepting a great deal from sundry gentlemen, nodded gravely.

'Will you be eating at home again tonight?' Mrs Timothy enquired. There was the faintest emphasis on the word 'again'.

'I'm going for a short walk and then I will get a cab over to Pa's house. You didn't cook anything special?'

'There are mutton chops,' Mrs Timothy informed her, 'but my back is not up to mutton chops though the improvement has been marked.'

'Right then! I will see you later,' Tansy said, and put on her cloak.

Outside, the rosy sky was tinged with purple-black clouds that scudded before the wind. It was still early though the light was fading, and there was the hint of rain in the wind.

On impulse she turned and walked down the narrow alley that bounded her back garden on to the river-bank. Despite the threat in the weather there were two or three elderly men seated with their fishing rods in their accustomed places.

She would sort out in her mind the facts she intended to lay before Laurence and then walk back to the main street and get a taxi cab. She would also, she decided, take a look at the little bridge. When she reached it she was rather touched to see that two large notices coloured in red were nailed firmly to both ends, announcing DANGER! BRIDGE DAMAGED. Underneath Robert Blake hadn't been able to resist writing his signature.

At least she could turn back without any fear of being plunged into the boiling Thames, she thought happily, casting a glance towards the leaping waves as the wind changed them into foam.

'Miss Clark! Miss Clark!'

She halted in surprise at the familiar voice and turned as William Benson hurried up to her, his drab overcoat flapping above his ankles, a deerstalker hat pulled down over his ears.

'Mr Benson, has something happened?' she enquired anxiously.

'Nothing further since we last spoke,' he said, slowing slightly and gasping for breath. 'I must confess that your words earlier today, your very logical summing up of the situation, cannot but impress your father who was, I understand, quite someone to be reckoned with in his time! Have you spoken to him yet?'

'I intend having supper with him in a little while,' Tansy said, pausing. 'Mr Benson, my father never issues definite invitations to me or anyone else but he keeps open house for the few people he sees. If you came with me to explain — '

'Miss Clark, you forget that I too am in breach of the law,' he said. 'I have not profited by it personally but — '

'I hardly think that your selling off a few items for charity comes into the same category as Carl Royston's crimes,' Tansy said.

'Nevertheless it has troubled my con-science, Miss Clark. I have always been a peaceable man not given to vicious or criminal conduct,' he said earnestly. 'Indeed, I was greatly troubled when you had your narrow escape on the bridge the other evening. You would certainly have been swept away if — '

'How do you know about the damaged bridge and my narrow escape?' Tansy asked sharply.

'I must have heard — ' he began.

'Do you know a young man called Robert Blake?'

'I can't honestly say that I do,' he confessed.

'Robert Blake was the only witness and he agreed to say nothing for fear of alarming my father or my servants.'

'There are notices on the bridge,' he hastened to point out.

'They do not state that Miss Tansy Clark narrowly escaped drowning there! How do you know, Mr Benson?'

There was a brief pause and then he gave a long shuddering sigh that seemed to emerge from the depths of his being.

'There are benches here and there set against the back walls of the houses, Miss Clark,' he said. 'Let us sit there for a few moments. What I must first do is apologize. I was never a violent man but I have twice launched an unforgivable attack on you — not out of malice but I knew you were your father's daughter. I had heard vaguely that you had helped him unofficially in a couple of matters in which he was interested in a professional capacity. When you came to the museum I guessed it would only be a matter of time before you uncovered — But my action on that first occasion was almost automatic. I saw you walking very close to the edge of the bank and impulse overcame caution. Nobody was more relieved than I was when, I saw from the shadow of the trees, you so heroically pulled yourself up to the bank again.'

'You were the one who damaged the bridge?'

'It was already beginning to rot. I merely hastened the process a little and went home without waiting to see what results would follow.'

'But you saw me coming along the path?'

'You are a distinctive figure, Miss Clark. I saw you from quite a distance off and stood in the deeper shadows. I was hoping you would turn back and then I heard the splintering of wood and a youth came running past me to help you. Fate, Miss Clark! I accept the dictates of fate.'

'But why? I don't understand,' Tansy said

in bewilderment. 'You were surely not acting on Mr Royston's behalf?'

'There is one man I loathe more than any other in the world,' he said, 'and that is Carl Royston, whose son stole his valuable coins and who so arranged it that my dear son was convicted of the deed. My Frederick died in prison but he left the letter the warder gave privately to me. I knew then that my post at the museum was nothing more than a bribe to keep me from any further investigations into the theft. I did nothing for there was no proof but it eased my mind to sell off certain items for charity. Carl Royston never visited. Few people ever visit. And then I had an assistant curator thrust upon me — Joseph Fanshaw A bright young man, Mr Fanshaw! He began to enquire rather too closely into the provenance of some of the artefacts in the museum. He had, like your good self, a feeling for the ancient and the genuine.'

'You killed him?'

'The poison was administered in a cup of tea — No, no, the tea you drank today was quite harmless.'

'Drowning being your method where I'm concerned,' Tansy said.

She could hear herself sounding flippant but everything seemed unreal, dreamlike. In a moment she would wake up and realize she had been peacefully asleep on her bed.

'Miss Clark, it was never my intention to harm anyone,' he said pedantically. 'I had in a way already connived at the injustice done to Frederick by keeping the post at the museum after I read his letter to me. I remained at my job, selling off a piece here and a piece there, and then Joseph Fanshaw came as assistant and he was, as I have just said, bright — noticing — too noticing! I began to watch him, to watch where he went. I feared he would tell Carl Royston what I was doing — or confide in a friend. And he had a friend, Miss Clark.'

'Brook Wilton?' she hazarded.

'Both men having been privately employed by Carl Royston to keep their eyes and ears open in case the stolen Vashti statuette surfaced again.' He nodded. 'Joseph Fanshaw was asking questions about the artefacts in the Royston Museum, suspecting that I was selling a few off here and there, I suspect. He was also in close and secret contact with — '

'With Brook Wilton over at the Kensington Museum.' Tansy nodded.

'Not Brook Wilton,' Mr Benson said. 'When I saw Mr Wilton I recognized him at once though it had been many years since I had laid eyes on him. Brook Wilton was

Benjamin Royston, Miss Clark. Carl Royston's son.'

'Who had killed — '

'Who as a child of four, already steeped in wickedness, had killed his own mother. His father had covered up the deed about which only he knew and kept the boy with him. And then he had shielded him again when the coins were stolen. And my son was convicted and died by his own hand! Royston sent his son abroad then but he supported him financially, of that I'm sure; used him to seek out certain valuables stolen from tombs and passed from hand to hand. Then he engaged him to work at the Kensington Museum — he holds a directorship there. Nobody remembered his son. Brook Wilton settled to his work but I knew him. Even after all those years I knew him though he had no recollection of me whatsoever! But I remembered him and I knew that it was my duty to avenge my dear son. The mills of God, Miss Clark. The mills of God!'

'But how did you — '

'Though I recalled him clearly he did not remember me at all. I doubt if he had even noticed me at Frederick's trial. I was unimportant, you see. It was very simple to buy antimony — I signed the poison register at the pharmacy with a false name — and then to slip it into the tea he was drinking during his lunch break at the Kensington Museum. Revenge would have been sweeter had I been able to tell him what I had done but there was still satisfaction in knowing that Carl Royston had failed to keep the monstrous offspring of himself and the woman called Vashti. Of course I knew nothing until lately of the original murder of the poor woman — Royston would never have harmed her. It was the son, Miss Clark, and since I had some antimony over and since Joseph Fanshaw was asking very awkward questions about the artefacts in the museum then it struck me as only fair to kill two birds with the same stone, so to speak.'

'And then you tried to kill me,' Tansy said.

Trying to make out his features in the darkness with only the faint light of the moon above the scudding clouds, she found it impossible to realize that this dour, respectable, elderly man had killed two people already and attempted twice to rid himself of a third.

'I repeat,' he said in a weary tone, 'that I am not a man of violence. However, when a moment of desperation comes then one acts out of character!'

'And now?'

The talking seemed to have tired him for

his shoulders were slumped and his voice was slightly husky but she wished she had remembered to bring her pistol with her.

'You will want to report your findings to your father and he will insist on passing them on to the appropriate authority,' he said tiredly. 'It makes no matter. I learned recently that I have a serious medical condition which makes it highly unlikely that I will ever stand trial. You must do as you deem fit, Miss Clark. I was never a violent man.'

With a feeling of incredulity she watched him rise, tip his hat courteously and walk back slowly along the river-bank, an older man whom few would notice once, let alone spare him a second glance.

She waited until she was certain he had reached the main streets and then she rose and followed him at a distance until, with a sense of great relief, she gained her own home again.

18

'And that,' said Tansy, ending her recital, 'is the full story.'

'A rum do all round,' Finn commented dourly. 'You oughtn't to have gone haring off on your own, Miss Tansy, chatting away with a man like Carl Royston and then telling it all to that William Benson!'

'I never for one moment thought he might be involved,' she protested. 'It was only when he let slip that he knew I'd almost fallen in the river a second time that I realized he must have been the one who pushed me the first time! My seeking work at the museum struck him as curious and when he learned that I was your daughter — well!'

'My reputation lingers,' Laurence said with satisfaction.

'So what now?' She looked from one to the other enquiringly.

'I reckon you tell the tale all over again to Mr Frank,' Finn said.

'You're expecting him?' She quelled the little leap of delight.

'I sometimes think as how there's gypsy blood in me,' Finn said solemnly, 'since I often can tell things before they happen; also I just took a look through the window and he's crossing the road. I'll let him in.'

'You and Frank haven't seen each other for a while,' Laurence said casually.

'A few days only,' she replied, equally casual, though her hand had moved to smooth down her mane of red hair.

'Everything satisfactory?' Laurence asked as Frank entered the room.

'All according to plan,' Frank said. 'Miss Harris is now happily engaged to be married.'

'So soon!' Tansy heard the dismay in her own tone but couldn't control it.

'Hardly soon!' Frank said. 'Her suitor has been courting her these past two years without actually asking the vital question! I was happy to squire her around and give him the impression that another hopeful suitor was hot on the trail! The ploy worked, I'm glad to say. Susan is engaged and I can resume my normal activities.'

'You never said anything!' Tansy exclaimed.

'I promised to say nothing,' he said. 'I knew you'd realize that there was some method in my sudden mad liking for her company! A sweet girl but with limited conversational gifts. I am exceedingly relieved to know her suitor has finally asked the all-important question. A nice young man, born to be ruled by women, I fear, but I'm sure they will be very happy together and I am equally relieved that he didn't challenge me to a duel or anything overly dramatic. Tansy, you look full of news.'

He was interrupted by a loud voice shouting from below, the sound coming through the open window in a blur of syllables.

'Rea all abaht it! Suicide in blabla late nigh news hot off th' press!'

'I'll go and see what's up,' Finn said. 'Let's hope it ain't war!'

The syllables were becoming clearer now and the newsboy evidently paused for breath.

'Suicide in Kensington! Millionaire shoots himself. Carl Royston — '

'Has shot himself,' said Finn returning, newspaper in hand.

'Let me see!' Laurence stretched out his hand.

'Print's still wet,' Finn warned. 'Special late night edition!'

'Which I might've scooped if I hadn't been delivering Miss Susan Harris into the arms of her loving fiancé!' Frank said, exasperated.

'Read it, Pa!' Tansy said.

'Headline is 'SUICIDE OF CARL ROYSTON',' her father said, taking the newspaper which had only two pages. 'Here we are! 'The millionaire, Carl Royston, was found dead, shot through the head, when his footman took his supper into him earlier this evening. A handwritten note found at his side stated that he found the loneliness and increasing infirmity of old age intolerable. Mr Royston, born Carl von Reuston in Vienna, inherited a fortune in South African mining shares from his late father and settled in London where he became a naturalized British subject. He built Royston Museum for his own use and speculated in several fields including stock breeding and the buying and selling of antiques and increased his original fortune considerably. A patron of the arts, he held directorships in several museums and art galleries and also founded the Royston Museum in Chelsea. He married Vashti Saig, a Persian lady, in his middle years. She later returned to her own people and Mr Royston reared their only son, Benjamin, who is believed to have died abroad'.'

'I missed a scoop there,' Frank said regretfully.

'Who gets all the money?' Finn enquired.

'It doesn't say. He very likely eased what remnant of conscience he had by leaving it to the nation, though he never did get the knighthood he craved,' Laurence said.

'I'm beginning to feel guilty,' Tansy confessed. 'I went to see him and practically forced a confession out of him.'

'I doubt if you can take credit for that,' her father said briskly. 'Men like Royston don't up and shoot themselves because a young woman came asking questions about a few bones. I reckon he had already decided to make an end of it. Don't forget, he knew Brook Wilton was his son. He knew that he and the other assistant curator had died in suspicious circumstances — he had no other relations, no real reason to go on. Even the Vashti statuette had eluded him. I also am positive he would never have spoken so frankly to you had he not already determined to put an end to it all. Frank, have you eaten? We had a bite earlier — '

'So did I,' Frank assured him. 'I delivered Susan Harris into the care of her now doting fiancé and treated myself to a steak and a glass of burgundy before I came on here.'

'What about William Benson?' Tansy asked. 'He killed two men.'

'And says he won't live to come to trial. Do you believe that?'

Tansy frowned slightly, picturing the dried-up appearance of the curator, his harsh cough which she had often heard echoing through the silent display rooms.

311

'I think,' she said slowly, 'that he would never have tried to put a stop to my investigations had he not known his time was limited.'

'He had already killed two men,' Laurence reminded her. 'My own feeling is that Mr Benson was the type of person who has murderous inclinations that may lie dormant over many years but emerge at last, rather like water bursting out of a dam when the dam is damaged.'

'You think we should say nothing?'

'Arrests and trials cost public money,' he said musingly. 'No, this is one case that we would do well to mark down as unsolved. It isn't as if I was ever approached officially to look into it though I confess that I harbour no very friendly feelings towards William Benson when I think of his twice trying to murder my only daughter!'

'On which loving note I'll take my leave,' Tansy said, getting to her feet.

'I'll take you home,' Frank said promptly.

'There's no need — ' she began.

'On the contrary, there's every need,' he said firmly, taking her cloak from Finn and draping it around her shoulders. 'William Benson may change his nasty little mind and take a pot-shot at you just in case you decide to talk to the powers-that-be and I've had no chance to talk to you for quite a while. Good night, sir! Finn!'

He armed her down the stairs with unusual gallantry and they crossed the road into the park where the leaves lay thickly now on the ground.

'It all seems so unfinished somehow,' Tansy said.

'Not really. Everything tidies itself up in the end even without involving officialdom,' he reassured her. 'Carl Royston is no loss to humanity though one can understand his wanting to protect his son, but his actions regarding his wife's body — it takes a cold-blooded man to do what he did!'

'The bones!' Tansy said suddenly. 'Frank, they are still inside Antonio. We cannot — '

'Antonio being the empty-headed Roman centurion?'

'Except for Vashti's remains,' she said.

'In the morning we'll go to the museum and talk to William Benson. If the poor devil's really dying, he'll be glad to have his mind relieved.'

'We,' Tansy said. The word had a pleasant sound.

'I've missed you, Tansy girl,' Frank said abruptly. 'If Susan Harris hadn't sworn me to secrecy about my pretended courtship of her you'd've had the full story by now, but I knew you wouldn't for one moment believe that I'd fall in love with a girl who doesn't think it's correct for a female to come straight out and tell a man exactly how she feels.'

'I'm sensible like that,' Tansy said modestly.

'Oh, very sensible!' Frank laughed suddenly. 'You take solitary walks along the river-bank when you know perfectly well that some person unknown has already tried to push you in! You beard a ruthless man in his own home and ask awkward question about his missing wife! Yes, I can give you the palm for good sense!'

'I inherit it from my father,' Tansy said with a chuckle.

'I wish I had known your mother,' Frank said suddenly. 'I reckon she must have been quite a lady of character!'

'She was gentle.' Tansy paused to recall. 'She was small and dainty and she had a brain as sharp as a dagger and a sense of humour as big as London itself, and she relished hearing about murders, particularly those my father was engaged in solving. She used to say that it was a dull week without even one murder in the newspaper! Yes, you would've liked my mother.'

'But not as well as I like her daughter,' Frank said.

They had reached the far gate of the park

near the cab-stand and she stopped to look at him, aided by the light from the street lamp. He was one of the few men to whom she could literally look up, one of the very few who had always made her feel feminine and desired though in the years she had known him he had never offered more than a brief embrace.

'Do you really mean that?' she asked.

'I don't usually say things I don't mean,' he retorted. 'Tansy, I seem to spend much of my time handing you in and out of cabs. Don't you think it's time we got in the same cab and went home together to the same dwelling place?'

'Are you — You're not making an unconventional proposition?' she asked.

'With Finn and your father around,' he replied. 'I wouldn't dare. Tansy, I've loved you for a long time and I've decided that it's simply stupid not to ask you to marry me. If I delay you'll be off looking into another mystery and I'll be dashing round London trying to get a scoop. Will you marry me?'

'Yes,' Tansy said simply. 'Yes, of course I will.'

For a moment she thought he was going to embrace her fervently but at that instant a nearby cabbie called out, 'Are you taking a cab or going to ride on moonbeams?'

'The lady is taking the cab,' Frank said. 'I have a newspaper column to write. Tansy girl, I'll see you at the museum first thing in the morning.'

He bent his head, kissed her swiftly and handed her up into the vehicle.

'Funny kind of proposal,' the cabbie remarked loudly.

'He's very practical,' Tansy said happily.

Not until she had paid the fare and entered the hall of her house did she realize that during the walk through the park she had not thought of Geoffrey once.

'Everything all right, Miss Tansy?' Mrs Timothy enquired, coming into the hall.

'Everything is just splendid,' Tansy said contentedly as she went up the stairs.

In the morning everything seemed so ordinary that she had a fleeting suspicion she had imagined the whole of the previous evening, but the sight of Frank outside the front door when she answered the bell on the way to breakfast catapulted her into the new reality. She and Frank were going to be married and —

'Why are you here so early?' she demanded in most unloverlike fashion.

'To ensure you didn't sneak off to the museum without me,' he said, kissing her on both cheeks.

'I've not had breakfast yet!' she protested.

'Neither have I,' he returned genially. 'We can eat after we've spoken to William Benson.'

'Mr Frank! How nice to see you!' Tilde exclaimed artlessly as she crossed the hall with a breakfast tray.

'You too, Tilde,' he returned genially. 'You get prettier every day.'

'Tilde will be twenty-one in a couple of weeks,' Tansy informed him. 'We've been thinking of getting up a small theatre party for the occasion. It's meant to be a surprise but it's as well to check whether or not a surprise will be welcome. I thought a musical show?'

'Oh, Miss Tansy,' Tilde broke in, 'I'd love to see something really romantic! My mother often said there was nothing to beat Shakespeare.'

'*Antony and Cleopatra* is on in one of the theatres off the Haymarket,' Frank supplied.

'Isn't that rather — ' Tansy began doubtfully but was interrupted by the eager Tilde.

'Serpent of old Nile,' she breathed. 'Other women cloy the appetite they feed upon but she makes hungry where most she satisfies. Oh I've read it but I've never seen it performed!'

'Let the tickets be my treat,' Frank said. 'Miss Tansy and I have to go out so you may eat whatever's on that tray yourself.'

'Yes, Mr Frank.'

Tilde looked slightly startled at the authoritative tone.

'Frank and I are going to be married,' Tansy said and whisked through the front door without waiting to find out whether or not Tilde dropped the tray.

They walked without speaking towards the museum, Frank obviously preparing to face another attack on her, Tansy suddenly feeling her confidence surging back as she glanced at her escort.

She had half expected to find the museum closed but it was open and William Benson sat as usual in his cubbyhole, betraying no surprise when he beheld her companion.

'Good morning, Miss Clark,' he said formally. 'I take it that you informed — '

'Only my father and Mr Cartwright,' Tansy said.

'Should your father decide to inform the authorities . . . ' He had risen, straightening his lean shoulders. 'I will not of course resist arrest but my doctor's verdict was very clear.'

'You have heard the news about Carl Royston?' Frank said.

'There are somewhat highly coloured

accounts in most of the leading periodicals. He has, it seems, left his fortune to the nation.'

He gave a dry, incredulous little chuckle.

'What will you do now?' Tansy asked.

It seemed impossible to believe, when she looked at the elderly figure, that he had nursed a murderous grudge in silence for so many years and finally allowed his pent-up fury to burst out against her and more subtly against the two assistant curators, one because of his past deeds and the other because he had begun to ask too many questions.

'I will continue to work here,' he said. 'It can only be a matter of weeks at the most. I hope you will accept my apologies for my actions on the river-bank, Miss Clark? The first was a genuine spur-of-the-moment impulse. I have something for you.'

He half-turned, lifted a small cardboard box and offered it to her.

'I'll take that,' Frank said promptly and protectively.

'It contains the bones that remain of a lady who must have been very beautiful in her time,' Mr Benson said. 'Perhaps they could be privately interred in some quiet place. I leave it to you. Good day to you both.' He sat down again within his cubicle and picked up a brochure.

'Tansy?' Frank took her hand and walked with her out of the museum.

'Are we doing the right thing?' she wondered as they moved away.

'Your father believes so and I'd back his judgement any day,' Frank said soberly. 'Or are you having sudden doubts about my suitability as a husband?'

'I think you will be a splendid husband!' she said robustly. 'I'm just astonished you've been patient for so long.'

'I had to get Geoffrey out of that red head of yours,' he told her, 'and memories take time to fade. Will a Christmas wedding suit you?'

'So soon? Frank, we haven't even decided where to live!'

'My bachelor chambers are somewhat drab and uncomfortable,' he said. 'Your house strikes me as a desirable residence even if it does contain rather too many signs of Geoffrey's taste in furnishing.'

'We could redecorate,' Tansy said promptly.

'Indeed we could and I suggest we begin drawing up colour schemes immediately,' he said, and suddenly swept her into an embrace. 'Tansy girl, I will live anywhere you choose provided you agree to marry me before Christmas! Will you?'

And bending his fair head he didn't wait for her reply.

★ ★ ★

The theatre lights flared up as the final curtain fell. In the stalls where the birthday party sat, there was a concerted burst of applause.

'That was beautiful,' Tilde said in a hushed voice. 'Oh, the way she spoke her last lines! Made me want to cry, honestly it did!'

At her side Robert Blake said, 'Those old Egyptians had some high-faluting speeches, didn't they?'

'Provided by Mr William Shakespeare,' Frank said, his hand caressing Tansy's hand on the finger of which an antique ring of silver and amber gleamed.

'It was all the fault of Enobarbus,' Finn declared as they began to file out. 'He'd no business to go selling carpets in the first place. What's your opinion, Mrs Timothy?'

'All I know is that I never laughed once,' Mrs Timothy said gently massaging the small of her back.

★ ★ ★

Laurence had been duly informed of everything that had transpired and had listened intently before issuing a verdict.

'Not entirely satisfactory. I like my criminals to receive their just desserts at the hands of the law but justice works in mysterious ways. Despite his vast wealth, Carl Royston could no longer face even the luxurious private world he'd created for himself, and William Benson — I see no point in dragging a dying man through the courts. A man who had violence buried deep within him — but not a natural killer. So, you and Frank have decided to marry. I am delighted for you both though with two strongly opinionated people I foresee rough seas ahead. I look forward to my first grandchild. Now go away and leave Finn and me to chew over all the facts again!'

Now, under a round October moon, Tansy and Frank walked soberly along the river-bank. In her hands she carried a small cardboard box. It had rained earlier but now the breeze was crisp and the damp fronds of grass danced and swayed along the rough path.

'The river is high tonight,' Tansy noted. 'The rain has swollen it.'

'And the current's running fast,' Frank said.

'Are we doing the right thing?' She paused abruptly, looking down at the little box.

'I think it's exactly the right thing,' Frank said, slipping his arm about her shoulders.

'Then God speed, Vashti.'

'And God bless,' Frank said soberly as Tansy knelt by the foaming water, took the lid of the box off and gently slid the yellowing contents into the river.

They seemed for a moment to hover on the surface like delicate sculptures of ancient ivory and then the water embraced them and they were engulfed.

'Let's walk back and get Mrs Timothy to brew up some coffee before you set off home,' Tansy suggested, allowing Frank to pull her to her feet.

'Correction! To my bachelor apartment,' he teased.

'But not,' said Tansy, putting her arms round his neck, 'for very much longer!'

We do hope that you have enjoyed reading this large print book.

Did you know that all of our titles are available for purchase?

We publish a wide range of high quality large print books including:
Romances, Mysteries, Classics
General Fiction
Non Fiction and Westerns

Special interest titles available in large print are:
The Little Oxford Dictionary
Music Book
Song Book
Hymn Book
Service Book

Also available from us courtesy of Oxford University Press:
Young Readers' Dictionary
(large print edition)
Young Readers' Thesaurus
(large print edition)

For further information or a free brochure, please contact us at:
Ulverscroft Large Print Books Ltd.,
The Green, Bradgate Road, Anstey,
Leicester, LE7 7FU, England.
Tel: (00 44) 0116 236 4325
Fax: (00 44) 0116 234 0205

Other titles published by
The House of Ulverscroft:

TRUMPET MORNING

Maureen Peters

The Petrie family live on a farm in Anglesey, North Wales. Grandfather Taid is a Revivalist preacher; his wife, Nain, an Irish gypsy who casts spells to annoy her husband. Then there is the aunt who's sworn off men forever, and another always ready for a lark. Also an uncle married to a wife who doesn't fit in, another whose marriage will benefit the farm, and the youngest facing a darker destiny in 1940 with Great Britain at war. As eleven-year-old Nell prepares for grammar school, and the shadows of war creep closer, comedy and heartbreak mingle in this story of a most eccentric family.

THE LUCK BRIDE

Maureen Peters

On the outskirts of a Romany camp, Abner, a gypsy, finds a new-born baby wrapped in a fine shawl. Named Kushti, meaning 'luck', she grows up to be a beautiful young woman. After Nahor, a half-Romany, saves Kushti from being raped, she falls in love with him. However, Abner reveals Nahor's threat to find and kill the man who had deserted his mother when she was pregnant. Because this is against Romany law, the young couple cannot marry. Then, when the tribe goes to London, Kushti's beauty attracts the attention of Edward IV and his court . . .

A CHILD CALLED FREEDOM

Maureen Peters

This novel, complete within itself, is the final part of a trilogy about the Malones. When Tansy Malone first looks into the eyes of Tom Wolf, she is swept by love. However, their ways seem fated to part, for Wolf is a half-breed Indian returning to his father's tribe, and Tansy has an elderly husband and a delicate sister, with whom she is setting out for the New World. A variety of experiences lie ahead as Tansy travels along the Sacramento Trail, towards California — and as she moves from the unthinking passions of a girl to full maturity, Tansy finds, at last, her true destiny.

TANSY

Maureen Peters

The first part of a trilogy about the Malones. Fifteen-year-old Tansy's family find her hard to understand, though all of them — practical Bridie, gentle Kate and her brothers, Pat and Seamus — love her. Raleigh Devereux, the English youth to whom Tansy first offers her heart, treats her as a plaything. Michael O'Faolain, for whom she has affection, but no love, never comprehends her yearnings for the freedom to be herself alone. Not until the failure of the potato crop does Tansy come face to face with reality — and with the complexities of her own nature.

KATE ALANNA

Maureen Peters

To escape the famine in Ireland, the Malone sisters — Kate and Tansy — take a ship to Liverpool. However, they find that the city stinks of corruption and violence, and is menaced by cholera. In the twisting alleys and crowded docks, Tansy fights for survival and a better life for her sister and herself. In this mid-Victorian world she meets many strange characters, who help or hinder her struggles. Then events take a sudden and surprising turn, and the future of the Malones blossoms.

THE VINEGAR TREE

Maureen Peters

The novel that completes the Vinegar trilogy. Culminating in the Second World War, the third in the Vinegar trilogy completes the story of the families of Elizabeth and Moira, the sisters who left their native Ireland to make their fortunes. Despite the estrangement of the two sisters, a bridge is built when Elizabeth's grandson escorts his aunt on a trip to the USA, now Moira's home. The link between the families grows stronger, giving Elizabeth new life and hope for the future.